Mollie McQueen is NOT Ruining Christmas

For Simon and Snoop.

All I want for Christmas is you two.

Chapter One

The sound of Christmas carols filled the night air as Mollie McQueen stuffed her mitten-clad hands into her pockets and trudged through the freshly fallen snow. The sky was black, the air was cold and the High Street was littered with frantic shoppers. The rows of glittering trees that lined the pavement were twinkling relentlessly, illuminating the dark sky with a dazzling show of light. Santa Claus was coming to town and there was nothing anyone could do to stop him.

Children were excitedly circling the must-have toys in the Argos catalogue, and their frazzled parents were frantically scouring the shops in a last-minute bid to find them. Supermarket trollies were overflowing with mince pies, and the Scrooges of the world had crawled under their rocks to ride out the festivities. Despite the unrelenting cold weather and inevitable scuffling over frozen turkeys, it really was the most wonderful time of the year.

Silently singing along to the carols, Mollie brushed a tiny snowflake off the tip of her nose and continued on her way. The lyrics everyone knew and loved had been ringing in her ears all day, and she was powerless to stop her lips from moving in time to the music. The city of London was always alive with an electric charm of possibility, but the festive season gave it a certain *je ne sais quoi* that was impossible to replicate the rest of the year.

Every building was dressed for the occasion, restaurants were offering mulled wine to all customers who walked through the door, and children were mischievously throwing snowballs when their unsuspecting parents weren't looking. The sparkling city was buzzing with the contagious magic of Christmas, making the many people who walked the frosty streets believe they had stepped inside a snow globe.

Mollie had lost count of the number of Rudolph jumpers she had passed, but she was yet to throw on a paper hat herself and sample a Greggs festive bake. Watching the numerous groups of partygoers belting out Christmas classics on the Tube had become a normal part of her daily routine, as had listening to her co-workers complain about the Heston Blumenthal stuffing selling out at their local supermarket. The resident Payne and Carter Elf on the Shelf had found himself in many precarious positions, and the staffroom was constantly being topped up with fresh boxes of Quality Street. The nuances Mollie loved to hate were in full swing, which could only mean that the big day was edging ever closer.

Coming to a stop outside a department store, Mollie peered into the window and took a moment to admire the stunning display. The impressive tree was decorated in thousands of glistening baubles, with each one shining brighter than the last. A string of fairy lights weaved between the many green branches, casting a warm glow over the swarm of shoppers who had stopped to stare at the picture-perfect scene. Hundreds of beautifully wrapped gifts were piled up around the trunk, and an assortment of lavish Christmas crackers was scattered amongst them.

There were just ten days to go until Christmas Day, but Mollie hadn't sent a single card, she hadn't purchased one gift, and she hadn't decked the halls with anything other than wet laundry. Come the first of December, the McQueen house usually resembled Santa's grotto. Red stockings would hang from the fireplace, his and hers advent calendars would be propped up on the mantlepiece, and the two sparkly polar bears bought by Mollie's mother would stand proudly on the windowsill.

This year, all was quiet on the Christmas front. The door was missing its usual wreath, the sprig of mistletoe was absent from the hallway, and the alcove in the living room was minus the retro tree that Mollie normally insisted on rolling out on the first day of December.

Positioned next to Mrs Heckles' heavily decorated house, Mollie's bare mews looked quite miserable indeed. It would be fair for anyone on the outside to think that the McQueens had lost their Christmas spirit, but that couldn't have been further from the truth. In fact, Mollie was more excited for Christmas than ever before. Her house might not have been alive with the glow of a million fairies, but Mollie's heart was bursting with anticipation for the festivities that lay ahead.

After a rather eventful year, Mollie decided that she would celebrate this Christmas without buying into an ounce of the commerciality that usually overshadowed the merry season. This wasn't because she had been hit with the humbug stick, quite the opposite. For just one year, Mollie wanted to celebrate the true meaning of Christmas. She wanted to be grateful for the people that were standing around the tree, not just the gifts that were under it. She wanted to enjoy the run-up to the big day without having to worry about pre-ordering a turkey, and without panicking that she had missed one of the neighbours off her Christmas card list.

Spotting tinsel on the shelves in September and receiving emails to book New Year's Eve parties in October had forever irritated Mollie. She had always believed that the trend of bypassing Halloween and Bonfire Night in a race to see the fat guy in a red suit took away from the sheer magic of the celebration we wait three hundred and sixty-five days to arrive. If the last twelve months had taught Mollie anything, it was that time is precious. Yesterday's history, tomorrow's a mystery and today is a gift, which is why we call it the present. Being the season to be jolly, Mollie's new mantra couldn't have been more fitting.

So far, Mollie's plans to strip Christmas back to basics had raised more than just one eyebrow, but as the days passed, she was simply becoming more content with her unconventional decision. While her co-workers were spending their lunch breaks fighting over the three-for-two gifts in Boots, Mollie was tucking into a pasta bake without a care in the world. She was actually able to look forward to having her friends and family in the same place at the same time, minus the stress of hosting the perfect Christmas. Or at least, what the rest of the United Kingdom perceived to be the perfect Christmas.

When Mollie first announced her alternative plans to her nearest and dearest, she received nothing but negative feedback. Max accused her of trying to ruin Christmas, Margot told her to chuck back a daily vitamin D pill in a bid to rediscover her Christmas spirit, and Mrs Heckles responded by singing Christmas carols through Mollie's letterbox at any given opportunity. Despite their grumbling, Mollie was hell-bent on seeing her plans through to the end. She was determined to prove to everyone that you *could* enjoy Christmas without falling victim to the endless marketing campaigns that emotionally blackmailed you into purchasing unnecessary gifts for people who would rather have a humble slice of Yule log.

For the first time in Mollie's life, she was throwing all of that out of the window. Without being consumed with the commerciality of the big day, Mollie hadn't just saved her sanity, she had managed to save herself a pretty penny too. Making handmade gifts for her loved ones had brought Mollie more satisfaction than any presents she had ever purchased. Rather than throwing a bunch of gift sets into her shopping basket and deciding who would get what later, Mollie had put time and effort into creating gifts that she believed her friends and family would be truly overjoyed to receive.

She could hear her dad singing along to the CD she had put together of his favourite songs, she could picture her mother wearing the paperclip earrings she had painstakingly made following a YouTube tutorial, and she hoped that Mrs Heckles would enjoy the tooth whitening powder she had created after one too many botched attempts. Mollie was yet to be convinced if Tiffany would be grateful for the air fresheners she made with the help of three supersized tampons, but she was of the opinion that one failed experiment out of the dozens she had attempted wasn't *too* bad.

In spite of the less-than-impressed reactions to her rather unsupported mission to recapture the true essence of Christmas, Mollie had found herself with a guest list like never before. From her parents and in-laws to Tim and Mrs Heckles, Mollie's no-Christmas Christmas was gathering more attendees every day. Considering the amount of complaints she initially received, Mollie was pleasantly surprised by the number of willing participants she had accumulated.

However, as much as Mollie wanted to believe that her guests were counting down the minutes until Christmas Day, no one had banged down her door in search of a golden ticket, and no one had squealed with joy when they realised they weren't going to be treated to a turkey with all the trimmings. The truth was that the majority of Mollie's guests had either signed up as a last resort or done so in a bid to lure Mollie away from paperclip earrings and towards breakfast mimosas.

The first to join the party were Margot and Jasper, who simply could not agree on whose family to spend Christmas Day with. After ten games of Rock Paper Scissors resulted in a draw, they subsequently decided to spend the holidays with Mollie and invited both sets of parents to join them. With her in-laws being too consumed with quaffing Bollinger and purchasing more from Harrods than they could carry, Mollie didn't think Max's parents had quite grasped the concept of her no-Christmas Christmas.

Her parents, on the other hand, had grabbed the idea and ran with it. Instead of wrapping each spindle on the staircase in buckets of tinsel, Heather and Lawrence gathered together every ounce of Christmas paraphernalia they could find and donated them to the local charity shop. Although she appreciated their enthusiasm, Mollie did wonder if they had taken things just a little too far.

At the opposite end of the spectrum, Mrs Heckles had enough Christmas decorations for all of Fulham. Despite spending the last twenty Christmases alone, Mrs Heckles was full of festive cheer. So much so, she had dedicated every given moment to coaxing Mollie into joining the Rudolph-jumper brigade. Little did Mollie's neighbour know that every attempt she made at persuading her to step beneath the mistletoe simply pushed Mollie further towards sanitary-based gifts for the home.

The look on elderly Mrs Heckles' face when Mollie invited her to spend Christmas with them was something Mollie would cherish forever. Knowing Mrs Heckles as well as she did, Mollie was very aware that Mrs Heckles wasn't the type of woman to show affection to anyone other than her cat, Misty. Needless to say, Mollie was rather taken aback when Mrs Heckles enveloped her in a huge bear hug. She quickly redeemed herself by informing Mollie that she could do with asking Santa for some Frizz Ease in her stocking, but still, the feeling Mollie got when Mrs Heckles wrapped her wrinkly arms around her was absolutely priceless.

Just like with Mrs Heckles, Mollie took great pleasure in inviting Tim to the party. With Heidi touring the Balearic Islands in search of the perfect premises to open her tantric sex retreat, Tim was facing the prospect of celebrating Christmas alone. The passing of his mother was still fresh in everyone's minds, meaning that Tim had been inundated with offers from friends who would have welcomed him with open arms. Touchingly, Tim had shunned the various invitations in favour of joining Mollie and Max for their alternative celebration, and the McQueens couldn't have been happier to have him around their table.

Having more mouths to feed than ever before, Mollie could only hope that her stripped-back version of the perfect Christmas would be well received by her army of guests. Finally tearing herself away from the window, she slipped her hands into her pockets and continued the journey home. With just ten days to go, Mollie was in a race against time to pull off the impossible, but as Alexander the Great once said... *there is nothing impossible to him who will try.*

Chapter Two

'What the hell is this?' Max asked, frowning in confusion as he dangled one of Mollie's tampon air fresheners over the coffee table.

Looking up from her position on the living room carpet, Mollie wiped her sticky hands on her jeans and reached for her glass of water.

'It's a Christmas gift for your mum.' She explained, smiling at the decorated tampon proudly. 'It's supposed to be an air freshener.'

'An air freshener?' Bringing the tampon to his nose, Max inhaled deeply. 'Oh, I suppose it does smell quite nice. It's a bit like those ridiculously expensive bath bombs you insist on using.'

'I definitely wouldn't recommend putting it in water.' Mollie mumbled. 'Do you think Tiff will like it?'

As she waited to hear Max's verdict on the homemade gift, Mollie turned her attention to the tin of Vaseline that was sitting on the carpet in front of her.

'Sure.' After a rather unconvincing delay, Max nodded hesitantly and brushed his sandy hair out of his face. 'Mum loves all presents, you know that. Just do what my dad does and leave the receipt at the bottom of the bag.'

'Considering that I made it myself, Max, they'll be no receipt with that one.' She said matter-of-factly. 'Or with this...'

Holding out the tin of Vaseline, Mollie wiped a smear of red lipstick from the lid before passing it to Max.

'This one's for Margot.' She explained, looking down at the mess she had made on the floor and attempting to hide yet another stain beneath her knee. 'It's a personalised lip balm. People pay a fortune for personalised cosmetics.'

'How is it personalised?' Max asked, cursing when he realised his hands were covered in pink jelly.

'I made it myself using Margot's favourite shade of lipstick.'

Clearing up the aftermath of her gift-making session, Mollie made a stab at rubbing the pink mark out of the carpet with her foot. 'It's completely unique. You literally cannot buy that anywhere in the world. Isn't that cool?'

'Very.' Max agreed, forcing enthusiasm as he turned the television on.

Recognising that he was being sarcastic, Mollie rolled up the newspaper she had been using in a failed attempt to protect the carpet and scowled.

'Well, even if she doesn't like it, it's the thought that counts.' She said confidently. 'It's not the size of the gift that matters, but the size of the heart that gives it.'

'That's lovely, Mollie, but what was the thought behind *this*, exactly?' Pointing to the embellished tampon, Max raised an eyebrow in amusement.

'That it would be easier to make than the crochet poncho I was considering?' She admitted sheepishly.

Laughing in response, Max placed the tin of Vaseline on the coffee table and moved along the sofa to make room for Mollie.

'While we are on the subject of gifts, what are *you* asking Santa for?' Mollie asked, sitting down next to him and letting out a yawn.

'A new Audi would be nice.' Draping an arm around Mollie's shoulder, Max stared into the distance thoughtfully. 'Or a Rolex...'

'You know the rules.' Mollie interrupted. 'This year, we are only exchanging gifts that can be made with our own hands.'

Rolling his eyes, Max picked up the television control and flicked through the channels before settling on Home Alone.

'I have to tell you, Mollie, I'm very surprised by your determination to go through with this whole *only handmade* idea.' He said, running his fingers along her arm. 'I seem to recall a certain anniversary when you didn't speak to me for three days after I presented you with a bunch of homegrown flowers.'

'Those weren't homegrown, Max!' Casting a frown in his direction, Mollie tucked her raven hair behind her ears and scoffed. 'You told me that you had scoured a meadow for wildflowers in order to create a bouquet that would represent our journey together. The reality was that you had ordered them from a discount website using a coupon you found at the Blue Fajita. You even gave yourself papercuts to add some depth to your deceit.'

'In my defence, the papercuts *did* come from the flowers.' Max retorted defensively. 'I cut my hands to ribbons trying to remove that price tag. Who puts a sale sticker on a thorny stem? It beggars belief. I should have put a complaint in.'

'You're digging yourself a deeper hole.' Mollie fired back, recalling the day that she found the invoice for said flowers in Max's jeans while doing the laundry. 'And for your information, roses are *not* wildflowers. Wildflowers are dogtooth violets, swamp milkweed and black-eyed Susans.'

'Black eyes and dog's teeth?' Max repeated, screwing up his nose. 'Personally, I'd rather have the cut-price roses.'

Shaking her head, Mollie looked over her shoulder as Elvis padded into the room and immediately began clawing the rug.

'So, does Elvis fall into the handmade category?' Max asked, reaching down and gently pulling the purring kitten away from the rug that he seemed intent on destroying. 'Because he might have a little trouble attempting craftwork with those lethal claws.'

'Actually, Elvis has been putting his destruction skills to good use lately.' Mollie replied smugly. 'This little guy has been making his own litter.'

'Is that so?' Not appearing convinced, Max looked down at Elvis sceptically.

'Once I have finished with the weekly newspaper, I prop it up against his scratching post and an hour later we have litter.' She explained. 'It's like magic.'

Since Mrs Heckles and Frankie solved the mystery surrounding Elvis and his hatred for his litter tray, shredded newspaper had become a staple in the McQueen house. The small fortune they had accrued from not purchasing ludicrously expensive high-end kitty litter had gone a long way towards paying for the crafts Mollie required to create her DIY Christmas gifts. Unfortunately for Mollie, she quickly discovered that stationery stores demanded a higher mark-up than most backstreet dealers.

'Interesting.' Max replied, picking up the tampon air freshener and swinging it over where Elvis was sitting. 'Do you think he could do that with these things?'

Before Mollie could respond, Elvis raised a single paw in the air and batted the unsuspecting tampon out of Max's hands. Within a matter of seconds, Mollie's handmade air freshener was reduced to nothing more than a pile of confetti on the living room floor.

'Well, I think that answers *that* question.' Max remarked, watching Elvis circle the tampon carcass. 'It smells so familiar. Is that your Jo Malone?'

'Do you really think I would soak a tampon in my beloved Jo Malone just for your mum to hang it from the rear-view mirror of her car?' Mollie grumbled, bending down to clear away the mess that Elvis had caused before quickly whipping her hand away when he took a final swipe. 'I used a bottle of cheap scent I found at the pound shop.'

'You expected my mum to put that in the Jag?' Laughing to himself, Max shook his head and stretched out his long legs on the sofa. 'She wouldn't even give me a lift last week because the ice on my shoes would ruin the wool mats she had imported from Italy.'

'Point taken.' Mollie conceded, unable to stop her lips from stretching into a smile. 'It was a terrible idea.'

'I'd love to disagree with you, but I'm going to put my neck on the line and say that tampon air fresheners are *always* a bad idea.' Max said decidedly. 'As are no-Christmas Christmases, but hey, what do I know?'

'You know how much this Christmas means to me.' Yawning into her sleeve, Mollie dropped her head onto Max's chest. 'Would it kill you to be just a little supportive?'

'Would it kill *you* to enjoy Christmas like you're supposed to?' Max replied quickly. 'Just take a look around this room, Mollie. What about this place says *Christmas* to you?'

Moving her eyes around the sparse living room, Mollie inhaled deeply and studied her surroundings. Max was right. Without the usual sparkle of the traditional Christmas decorations, it did look rather bare. She couldn't deny that the walls were screaming out for a touch of glitz and glamour, but that presumption simply reinforced to Mollie what she was trying to do.

'Just imagine a few lights across the mantlepiece.' Max whispered into her ear. 'Maybe a Christmas tree by the window, a couple of stockings over the fireplace and possibly a gift or two.'

'But that's how it begins.' Not being fazed by Max's protest, Mollie allowed the sleeves of her knitted jumper to fall over her hands. 'Once you allow that through the door, you're on a roller coaster to the North Pole.'

'I appreciate the sentiment behind what you're trying to do.' Max continued gently, his grey eyes softening as he looked at Mollie. 'All I am saying is that you *could* get your message across *and* allow everyone else to enjoy Christmas at the same time.'

'And everyone *will* enjoy Christmas!' Mollie replied confidently. 'You might not believe it right now, Max, but our guests will enjoy this Christmas more than any other. You just wait and see.'

Casting a doubtful glance at the grubby Vaseline tin, Max chose to remain silent.

'Maybe I have missed the mark with a few of my gift ideas.' Mollie admitted, following Max's gaze to the coffee table. 'But Christmas isn't about receiving expensive gifts. It's about being grateful for what we already have.'

'Isn't that the meaning of Thanksgiving?' Max asked. 'I thought the meaning of Christmas was to bring the greatest happiness to others, and the greatest joy to me would be a new set of wheels.'

'You don't have a *set of wheels* to begin with!' Mollie giggled and pulled the sofa throw over their legs. 'I completely understand your apprehension, Max, but you really don't need to worry.'

Reluctantly nodding, Max smiled when Mollie planted a kiss on his cheek and turned up the volume on the television.

'Trust me. Everything is in hand.' She whispered. 'Just for this one year, let go of what you believe Christmas should look like and embrace it for what it is...'

Chapter Three

Struggling to keep her balance as she made her way up an extremely wobbly set of ladders, Mollie cautiously placed the ancient angel on the highest branch of the Christmas tree. The enormous tree swayed from side to side as Mollie fought to ensure the topper was securely in place. Not daring to breathe until she was certain it was in the perfect position, Mollie slowly removed her hands.

'It's not straight!' Mrs Heckles yelled, batting Mollie's leg with the end of her walking stick and almost knocking her off the ladders in the process. 'You need to move it to the left!'

Grabbing the handrail before she took a tumble, Mollie narrowly avoided a festive trip to A&E.

'Mollie, can you hear me up there?' Mrs Heckles continued. 'You need to move it to the left!'

Gritting her teeth, Mollie cursed beneath her breath as she strived to place Mrs Heckles' fifty-year-old tree topper in a completely straight position.

'Is that right?' She asked, looking down at Mrs Heckles and scowling when her neighbour shook her head. 'More to the left?'

'Yes.' Mrs Heckles instructed bossily. 'More... more... more... keep going... no... back to the right... to the right... there. Stop! *Stop!*'

Doing as she was instructed, Mollie cautiously took a step down the ladder before pausing when the angel wobbled slightly.

'Easy!' Mrs Heckles hollered, glaring at Mollie from her position next to the old gas fire. 'For heaven's sake, don't ruin it now! It's taken you forty-five minutes to get the damn thing up there! Misty could have done it in less time!'

Resisting the urge to topple the entire tree over in retaliation, Mollie pursed her lips and carefully made her way down the rickety set of ladders. Once back on the safety of Mrs

Heckles' living room carpet, Mollie took a step backwards and looked up at the giant Christmas tree. Being far too tall for Mrs Heckles' ceiling to cope with, the immense tree was leaning over on one side, creating a low arch over Mollie's favourite armchair. The incredible number of dated baubles and flashing lights it was carrying only served to weigh it down even more. So much so, Mollie was counting down the seconds until it gave way completely.

'Doesn't it look fantastic?' Mrs Heckles exclaimed, smiling at the tree proudly. 'You just can't beat the smell of fresh pine, can you?'

Giving her neighbour a sideways glance, Mollie nodded politely. Between the scent of the dozen gingerbread candles that were burning and the overwhelming stench of sherry, Mollie was surprised that Mrs Heckles could smell anything at all. Considering that she had somewhat of a reputation for being a grumpy grouch, Mrs Heckles' love for Christmas had completely taken Mollie by surprise. From the incredible collection of singing snowmen that were dancing on the sideboard to the obscene number of Christmas cards that were adorning the walls, Mrs Heckles was one step away from throwing on an elf costume and asking the children of the neighbourhood if they had been naughty or nice.

'I must admit, Mrs Heckles, I didn't have you down as Santa's little helper.' Mollie mused, straightening a bauble on the tree and wincing when the branch groaned loudly. 'I would have put money on you being quite the Scrooge.'

'You cheeky monkey.' Mrs Heckles retorted. 'Christmas is the most wonderful time of the year!'

Raising an eyebrow, Mollie smiled as Mrs Heckles clapped her hands together and the gang of snowmen erupted into yet another rendition of Rockin' Around the Christmas tree.

'There are parties for hosting, marshmallows for toasting, and it's perfectly acceptable to drink at all hours of the day.' Fluffing up her freshly permed hair, Mrs Heckles shuffled into the kitchen before returning with a decanter and two glasses. 'Sherry?'

'Mrs Heckles, your blood pressure is going to be through the roof.' Mollie protested, remembering that her neighbour was due for her annual blood pressure check. 'We all like to let our hair down at Christmas, but don't be making a habit of this...'

'I think you'll find my blood pressure is just fine.' Mrs Heckles interrupted defiantly. 'I'm fit as a fiddle.'

Struggling to believe that a woman who consumed more rum than a sailor and, until recently, lived on a diet of wine gums and sugar-loaded tinned fruits had anything but appalling blood pressure, Mollie narrowed her eyes suspiciously.

'I'm telling you! I had my blood pressure checked by the doctor just last week. I'm strong as an ox.' Waving the sherry in the air, Mrs Heckles crossed her fingers behind her back. 'So, are you joining me or not?'

Looking at her watch, Mollie decided that it was five o'clock somewhere and gave Mrs Heckles a brief nod. As Mrs Heckles began to pour the amber nectar out of the decanter, Mollie took a second glance at the glasses.

'Mrs Heckles, you do know that those aren't sherry glasses, don't you?' She said, eyeing up the tumbler hesitantly. 'You might want to go easy on...'

Mollie promptly stopped talking when Mrs Heckles proceeded to fill both glasses up to the brim.

'I hope you don't use the stairlift after drinking this stuff.' Mollie mumbled, tentatively pulling the tumbler towards her and taking great care not to spill a drop. 'If I had it my way, sherry would only be in trifles.'

'I recall you saying that rum should only be in daiquiris before you sampled one of my famous rum teas.' Mrs Heckles said knowingly, motioning for Mollie to try the sherry. 'Now you can't get enough of them.'

To say that Mollie *couldn't get enough* of her friend's rather odd choice of cocktail wouldn't quite be true. After spending months ridiculing Mrs Heckles' habit of lacing her PG Tips with a hefty dose of Bacardi, Mollie finally decided to give it a go for herself. Despite not particularly enjoying the strange offering, she managed to make her way through it and successfully resisted the urge to vomit.

Unfortunately for Mollie, her silent reaction was misconstrued by Mrs Heckles as dumfounded joy. As such,

Mollie now had to grin and bear a mug of Mrs Heckles' special brew at least once a week. With Christmas on the horizon, Mrs Heckles seemed to have abandoned her love for rum in favour of throwing back sherry like there was no tomorrow, giving Mollie the get-out-of-jail-free card she desperately needed.

Attempting to bring the glass to her lips without recoiling, Mollie took a sniff of the sherry and grimaced.

'That'll put hairs on your chest!' Wiping her lips on a lace handkerchief, Mrs Heckles chuckled as she watched Mollie gather the courage to take a tiny sip.

'I don't doubt it.' Mollie replied, spluttering as the alcohol burned the back of her throat. 'Don't go too close to the fire.'

'I don't think there's much chance of that, do you?' Cocking her head towards the fireplace, Mrs Heckles sighed fondly. 'Just look at her...'

Following her gaze, Mollie smiled at the sight of Misty curled up into a ball on the garish rug. Her pink nose was buried into her paws, and her furry tail was wrapped tightly around her body. Judging by the string of gold tinsel on her collar, Misty had also been hit with Mrs Heckles' Christmas stick.

'So, what will Misty be getting in her stocking this year?' Mollie asked, taking a seat in her favourite armchair and frowning when a bauble hit her on the head.

'A lot more than you will be getting at this rate.' Mrs Heckles fired back, giving Mollie an accusing look over the rim of her glass. 'I take it you're still stuck on your Scrooge Christmas idea?'

'It's not a *Scrooge Christmas*, Mrs Heckles.' Mollie replied, struggling to see her neighbour through the many hanging branches. 'It's still Christmas, just without all of *this*...'

Motioning to the tree that was blocking her view, Mollie laughed when a candy cane fell into her lap.

'I wouldn't eat that.' Mrs Heckles warned. 'I've been rolling out that same pack of candy canes since the eighties.'

Tactfully placing the sticky decoration on the nest of tables, Mollie wiped her hands on her jeans.

'What did Christmas look like in the eighties?' She asked, settling into her seat as Mrs Heckles changed the television channel with the end of her walking stick.

'Exactly the same as it does now, just with more foil decorations and prawn cocktails.' Resting her vast glass of sherry in her lap, Mrs Heckles pointed at the string of foil decorations that were dancing above her head. 'Unless you're in this house where foil decorations and prawn cocktails are still all the rage.'

'How about when you were a child?' Mollie persisted. 'I bet it wasn't so materialistic back then?'

'Materialistic? You must be joking!' Letting out a deep chuckle, Mrs Heckles tipped back her head and smiled as she thought back to her childhood. 'When I was a young girl, the most I would get under the tree was a satsuma. If I was extremely lucky, a Mars bar too.'

'A Mars bar?' Mollie repeated cynically. 'Just to clarify, that did mean the same back then as it does today?'

'It did indeed, but this wasn't any old Mars bar.' Mrs Heckles explained, her eyes glistening as she spoke. 'This Mars bar might as well have been made of pure gold. I would watch with bated breath as my old man took the sharpest knife from the kitchen and cut that bar into twelve tiny slices. From Christmas Day to the fifth of January, my mother would leave one of those slices on my pillow.'

Braving another sip of sherry, Mollie closed her eyes for a moment and imagined herself as a fly on the wall in Mrs Heckles' story.

'These days, children eat chocolate as an everyday occurrence, but back then it was like finding treasure. I made that single slice of chocolate last for an hour. I would nibble the edges until only the centre remained, and when I could nibble no more, I held the nougat on my tongue until it disappeared.'

Completely transfixed by the sound of Mrs Heckles' voice, Mollie peeled open her eyes and smiled.

'It wasn't a PlayStation or one of these fancy phones, but the feeling I got when I raced into the bedroom to discover one of those little pieces of chocolate has never been paralleled to this very day.' Mrs Heckles continued wistfully. 'It's really quite amazing that such an insignificant amount of chocolate could evoke such a strong reaction. That it could bring so much joy and happiness to a person, but it did. It really did.'

As Mrs Heckles stared longingly into the fire, Mollie felt a warm glow wash over her.

'You have no idea how much I want to bottle every word you have just said.' Mollie replied, suddenly springing to life. 'That is *exactly* what I am trying to get back to. We've lost that magic. The excitement of the unknown has long gone. We write lists of the things that we want and return the things that we don't. We send Christmas cards without paying any attention to the words that we write inside, before tossing the ones we receive into the recycling bin the second the calendar flips over to January. We simply go through the motions without putting any thought into why we are actually doing them.'

'I can't argue with that.' Nodding along, Mrs Heckles glanced at her own collection of Christmas cards. 'My friend, Brenda, she doesn't even bother writing her cards out anymore. Her daughter in New Zealand prints out the names and addresses and posts them to her. She even downloads a festive message from the spider's web to go inside.' Shaking her head, Mrs Heckles took a big gulp from her glass. 'The complimentary card from Street Cars has more emotion in it. At least theirs is handwritten. And they throw in a discount voucher for January, which is more than I can say for Brenda. She's tighter than a duck's...'

'That's another great point.' Mollie interrupted, before Mrs Heckles could turn the air blue. 'We're like puppets. We have fallen into a routine of putting on a display purely because that's what we're expected to do at Christmas. Why can't we rewrite the rules and decide our own Christmas celebrations?'

'I'm afraid you're on your own with that one.' Mrs Heckles retorted, turning her attention to the television. 'The more traditions the merrier, I say. Now can you be quiet for a minute? Nigella's Christmas Kitchen is about to start!'

'Let me guess.' Mollie muttered, kicking off her shoes and relaxing in the armchair. 'Turkey, sprouts and cranberry sauce?'

'Absolutely. It wouldn't be Christmas without it...'

Chapter Four

'Secret Santa.' Joyce grumbled, sighing heavily as she came to a stop in front of Mollie's desk. 'Maximum spend is ten pounds. No alcohol and no perishables.'

Looking up from her computer, Mollie smiled at the sight of the Payne and Carter receptionist holding out an enormous Santa hat. Her usual grouchy expression was in full force, but in place of her name tag was a flashing snowman brooch.

'If you happen to pull my name out of the hat, you should know that I'm lactose intolerant. I spend Christmas alone, so there isn't anyone I can regift to. Chocolates and anything else containing dairy would be a complete waste of money.' Joyce said bluntly, shuffling forwards and offering the red hat to Mollie. 'But if you follow the rules on no perishables, that shouldn't really be an issue.'

The sound of phones ringing filled the silence as Mollie tried to think of a polite way to decline Joyce's invite to the Secret Santa party.

'Thank you, Joyce, but I don't think I'm going to participate in Secret Santa this year.' She replied, smiling brightly. 'Sorry.'

Keeping her frown firmly in place, Joyce didn't move a muscle. Her grey curls and oversized glasses framed her angry face, completing her tried-and-tested Mrs Doubtfire look perfectly.

'Did James cut your wage?' Joyce asked, her sullen tone of voice indicating that she didn't care either way. 'Is that why you haven't signed up to the Christmas party? I couldn't help noticing that your name wasn't on the list.'

Taken aback by Joyce's unusual level of observance, Mollie shook her head.

'No. It's nothing to do with money. It's...'

'Don't you celebrate Christmas?' Joyce interrupted glumly. 'Are you a Buddhist like that pretty girl in HR?'

'I'm not a Buddhist, and I *do* celebrate Christmas.' Mollie confirmed. 'It's just...'

'If you're worried about getting Arnold, the odds are against it.' Resting her spare hand on her hip, Joyce peered into the hat. 'There must be over twenty names left in here.'

As Joyce offered her the hat once more, Mollie realised that it would be far easier to take part in the office tradition and wave Joyce on her way than it would be to explain her no-Christmas Christmas to her.

Deciding to take one for the team, Mollie finally conceded.

'Fine.' She said, offering the cranky receptionist a friendly smile. 'Count me in.'

Without saying a word, Joyce began to shake the hat at a snail's pace.

'Are you giving them a good shuffle?' Mollie asked, pressing the divert button on her desk phone when it rang.

'They're already mixed.' Joyce replied expressionlessly. 'I'm just building the momentum.'

Staring back at Joyce's deadpan face, Mollie pursed her lips and waited patiently until Joyce gave her the nod.

'Here goes...' Sticking her hand into the hat, Mollie twirled her fingers around the many strips of paper before pulling out a name and dropping it onto her desk. 'Ta-dah!'

'We'll be exchanging the gifts at the Christmas party this Friday.' Joyce announced. 'I'll put your name on the list. Remember, no perishables.'

Before Mollie could respond, Joyce sloped away and resumed jiggling the hat. Shaking her head, Mollie reached for her cup of coffee and frowned when she realised it was empty. After locking her computer screen, she dropped the folded strip of paper into her handbag and made her way to the staffroom.

'Slease!' Mollie exclaimed happily, pausing in the staffroom doorway when she discovered Tim sitting at one of the tables. 'What are you doing up here?'

Wearing a yellow paper hat and a badge that read *Kiss me, it's Christmas*, Tim grinned widely as he tucked into what appeared to be a chicken leg. His blue shirt was accessorised with a novelty Santa tie, which was erratically flashing like a broken traffic light.

'Molls!' He cheered. 'How the devil are you?'

'I'm not bad, Slease.' Stepping into the room, Mollie rinsed out her cup before placing it beneath the coffee maker. 'Have you been collared by Joyce yet?'

'I have indeed.' Holding up a strip of paper, Tim waved it around proudly. 'I got Austin. Who did you get?'

'Tim!' Mollie laughed and sat down in the seat next to him. 'The whole point of Secret Santa is that you don't tell anyone who you are buying for!'

Seemingly stumped, Tim lowered his arm and cleared his throat.

'Well, I won't tell *him* who I got.' He replied slowly, tearing up the paper and dropping it into the bin before anyone could see the evidence. 'Besides, it may have said Austin, it may have said James, Arnold, Molls or Joyce. Who knows?'

'*I* know.' Mollie said. 'Because you just told me.'

'Ah!' Wagging a finger knowingly, Tim returned to his chicken leg. 'But did it? Maybe I was bluffing. You know how good my poker face is.'

From the few games of poker the gang had played together, Mollie knew that Tim's poker face was absolutely terrible. Not only did he tap his nose when he got a good hand, but he was also the only person Mollie had ever met who mouthed his cards to himself as he waited his turn.

'So, I take it you're going to the Christmas party this Friday?' Mollie said, collecting her mug when the coffee machine beeped. 'To give Austin his present?'

'Of course I am!' Wiping his hands on a napkin, Tim pushed his paper hat up his forehead when it fell in front of his eyes. 'I wouldn't miss...'

Tim's voice trailed off into silence as Mollie raised her eyebrows.

'I see what you did there, you sneaky Pete.' He chuckled. 'But seriously, I wouldn't miss the chance to see Austin Carter throwing some shapes on the photocopier for all the cider in Somerset.'

'Really?' Mollie asked, struggling to envisage her strait-laced boss letting his hair down.

'Really!' Tim repeated. 'Last year, he started a conga line in reception and threw up before we reached the boardroom! That guy is crazy after a few pints of mild.'

Knowing that the boardroom was just a few feet away from her desk, Mollie screwed up her button nose as she recalled the carpet randomly being changed in January.

'*Anyway...*' She said, trying to remove the image of her boss hurling behind the vending machine from her mind. 'If you're going to the party, would you mind taking my Secret Santa gift along?'

'Sure.' Tim replied, struggling to fasten his Tupperware box. 'But why can't you take it? You *are* going, right?'

Blowing into her mug, Mollie shrugged her shoulders and prepared herself for Tim's protest.

'Come on, Molls!' Tim cried, his face falling with disappointment. 'Everyone's going to be there!'

'*Everyone* being...'

'Me, Austin, James, Joyce and, you know, the other eighty-nine members of staff that work here.' Trying to make the party sound as exciting as possible, Tim removed his paper hat and placed it on Mollie's head. 'You have to come.'

Being very aware that eighty-nine members of staff was a bit of a stretch, Mollie pulled the bowl of chocolates from the centre of the table towards her.

'I don't know, Tim.' She said tentatively. 'You know I've been trying to avoid all the tacky Christmas traditions this year.'

'Tacky?' Tim echoed in horror. 'You *did* hear my conga story, didn't you?'

Nodding in response, Mollie smiled when she spotted the Elf on the Shelf warming his bum on the toaster with his trousers around his ankles.

'A Christmas party is the gateway to turtle doves and a partridge in a pear tree.' Mollie replied wisely. 'I don't need to see James and Austin making fools of themselves in order to enjoy Christmas.'

'Please come, Molls. It won't be the same without you.' Tim persisted, clearly not willing to give up just yet. 'If you can't come for the free booze, do it for me. That can be your gift to me.'

Suddenly remembering that Tim was the only one in her group that she hadn't yet made a Christmas present for, Mollie saw an opportunity to cross something else off her list.

'Fine. I'll go.' Shooting him a smile, Mollie clinked her mug against Tim's water bottle. 'Merry Christmas!'

Cheering loudly, Tim fist-pumped the air.

'Will you wear a Christmas jumper?' He asked hopefully. 'I happen to have a spare one. It's a bit grubby around the edges, but it still does the job.'

'Don't push it, Slease.'

Begrudgingly accepting this, Tim turned his attention to his phone as the pair of them fell into a comfortable silence. Flipping through Tim's newspaper, Mollie dived into the bowl of chocolates and popped one into her mouth.

'Chocolate liqueur?' She asked, pushing the chocolates towards Tim.

Automatically reaching into the bowl, Tim paused before shaking his head.

'Actually, I better not.' He said. 'I'm going to be driving later.'

'One brandy chocolate isn't going to send you over the limit!' Laughing out loud, Mollie tossed him a foil-wrapped chocolate.

'It's no laughing matter, Molls.' Immediately throwing it back, Tim shook his head seriously. 'I once watched a show where a woman lost her license from having one too many bourbon balls. Those things should come with a warning.'

Not being convinced, Mollie unwrapped another chocolate and returned to the newspaper.

'Oh, while we are on the subject of Christmas, I did have a favour to ask you.' Tim said suddenly, placing his empty Tupperware box into his backpack.

'It was only a few seconds ago that I agreed to the last favour you asked of me.' Mollie replied, blowing into her mug of coffee once more.

'I think you will find that your attendance at the Christmas party is a gift.' Tim corrected. 'A favour is quite different from a gift. I think the Oxford dictionary's definition of a favour is...'

'Slease, I'm kidding.' Mollie interrupted gently. 'Go ahead.

What can I do for you?'

Resting his elbows on the table, Tim cleared his throat before speaking.

'As you are aware, this is the first Christmas since mum... you know.' He said slowly. 'And I was hoping that you might possibly be able to do something for me in her memory.'

'Anything.' Mollie replied, wanting to make Tim's first Christmas without Dottie as enjoyable as it could possibly be. 'Anything at all.'

'This might seem trivial to you, but there wasn't a Christmas that went by without Mum mixing beans into the mashed potatoes.' Tim said, his cheeks flushing. 'It was a Slease family tradition that I was hoping to continue wherever I went.'

'Okay...' Mollie said slowly. 'Just to be clear, you're talking about tinned beans here?'

'I certainly am.' Tim confirmed. 'Just good old baked beans.'

'Mashed potatoes and baked beans.' Mollie said to herself. 'How did that happen, exactly?'

'It all started as a mistake. You see, we always had peas in our mashed potatoes, but one year, when my dad was still around, he had one too many ciders and opened the wrong can. Once he realised his mistake, it was too late.' Laughing at the memory, Tim shook his head and exhaled loudly. 'After that, we did it every year. Christmas just wasn't Christmas without beans and mash.'

Staring into space wistfully, Tim composed himself when he realised that Mollie was staring at him.

'You think it's silly, don't you?' He said.

'Not at all.' Mollie replied quickly, really hoping that Tim wasn't going to be majorly disappointed with her unconventional celebration. 'It's just... you do know that we aren't having a traditional Christmas lunch, don't you?'

'Don't worry, Molls, I can't wait to experience your Christmas with a twist. I was just hoping that you could maybe slip the beans and mash in there at some point.' A flash of sadness hit Tim's eyes before he replaced it with a smile. 'It's really not a problem if you can't. I just thought it was worth asking. As Mum used to say, *if you don't ask, you don't get.*'

As much as Mollie wanted to stick to her guns and decline

every tradition that came her way, she couldn't see any harm in granting Tim his rather simple Christmas wish. Besides, between Mrs Heckles' rum-polluted teas and Tim's frankly odd take on mashed potatoes, it seemed Mollie's Christmas was going to be anything *but* traditional.

'Beans and mash it is.' She said warmly. 'Consider it done.'

Chapter Five

Strolling past the rows of wooden stalls and busy food trucks, Mollie waited patiently while Margot stopped to admire yet another selection of glitzy trinkets. The black sky was littered with stars, but even the dazzling display of astronomy couldn't distract Mollie from the fact that she couldn't feel her toes. In temperatures even penguins would deem to be too cold, she and Max were perusing the Christmas market with Margot and Jasper, but Mollie had spent the majority of her time at the mulled wine station. With the mercury dropping below freezing, saving herself from frostbite was her main concern.

Due to her decision not to purchase any gifts this year, Mollie had found herself wandering around rather aimlessly. While Margot acquired more bags than poor Jasper could carry, Mollie could only offer words of discouragement. Her attempts at persuading her sister that she didn't need to buy eye-wateringly expensive tea towels purely because they had snowflakes printed on them fell on deaf ears, as did her efforts at luring Jasper away from the traditional Christmas dinner.

Apparently, the idea of not tucking into a dressed bird on the big day was worse than not celebrating at all. As far as Max's brother was concerned, it seemed that he genuinely didn't care what was waiting for him under the tree. For him, it was all about what was on his plate, and what was on Jasper's plate come Christmas Day hadn't changed in thirty years.

From the perfectly basted turkey to honey-roasted vegetables and sprouts cooked with salty cubes of bacon, all Jasper had talked about was his love for the classic festive lunch. With Mollie planning an alternative offering, every time the word *turkey* fell out of Jasper's mouth she became more concerned that he was going to be hugely disheartened when he was presented with his meal on Christmas day.

'By the way, what *are* we having for Christmas dinner?' Jasper asked, as though reading Mollie's mind. 'Your whole anti-Christmas thing isn't going to extend to the food, is it?'

'Anti-Christmas.' Mollie repeated. 'That's a new one.'

'You should hear what my mum calls it.' Brushing back his blonde hair, Jasper scratched his stubble-clad jaw.

'What does she call it?' Mollie asked, genuinely intrigued.

'I can't repeat it here, Mollie!' Jasper exclaimed. 'There are children around!'

Rolling her eyes, Mollie laughed and shook her head. As dramatic as she was fabulous, her mother-in-law was never going to understand the method to Mollie's apparent madness. Tiffany McQueen had always been the type of woman who threw her credit card to the wind and paraded along Bond Street in search of mountains of useless tat. Her tree was decorated by a specialist company from the city, and her food was delivered from an artisan shop on Christmas Eve.

On paper, Tiffany's Christmas couldn't have been more perfect than if it was pulled from the pages of a Fortnum and Mason brochure. But behind the glitz and glamour of the big day was a whole load of nothing. The main motivation pushing Tiffany to have such a spectacular celebration was to keep up with the Joneses. It would be fair to say that the worst thing to happen to Tiff over the festive period was discovering her neighbours had erected a pair of light-up reindeers outside that were twice the size of hers.

'So, come on then.' Jasper said, popping Mollie's thought bubble. 'What are we going to be eating?'

'I... I thought I would keep that as a surprise.' Looking up at her brother-in-law, Mollie smiled and hoped her innocent expression would be enough for him to drop the subject. 'We all like surprises, don't we?'

'It's going to be that bad, huh?' Jasper replied teasingly. 'Please tell me it's not vegetarian. I tried to go vegetarian back in April and I nearly passed out after two weeks.'

Giggling at Jasper's crestfallen face, Mollie shook her head and tugged her handbag onto her shoulder.

'Is it worse?' Shivering as he zipped up his parka coat, Jasper exhaled into the cold air. 'Is it vegan?'

'It's not vegan.' Mollie revealed, much to Jasper's relief. 'The truth is that I haven't come to a final decision as to what exactly we shall be serving, but I do have a shortlist that I am toying with.'

'Is turkey anywhere on that list?' Jasper asked hopefully, his nose twitching as the smell of freshly baked mince pies floated past.

'There will be no turkey, but you shall be treated to a feast like no other.' Mollie replied. 'I promise.'

As Jasper hung his head, Mollie bit her lip guiltily. She was very aware that no matter how you chose to celebrate Christmas, the crescendo of the day was always the food. The meal that makes you loosen your belt and dab your forehead with a napkin after finally completing it had forever been the highlight of Mollie's Christmases, hence why she was having the hardest time deciding what to serve. Her grandmother taught her that you should always treat guests in your home as though they are royalty, and that rule was only amplified during the festive season.

Trying to act on her grandmother's famous mantra, Mollie had found herself browsing the web in search of non-traditional recipes. Her online research opened a Pandora's box full of weird and wonderful ideas that Mollie wasn't sure she was brave enough to try. From replicating the Elizabethans and proffering Lambswool cocktails, to mimicking the Georgians and attempting to turn her hand to a Twelfth Night cake, the options available to Mollie were endless, but not one of them made her mouth water in the way that turkey and trifle did. Plus, judging by the conversation she had just shared with Jasper, bean-laced cake and drinks that resembled sheep shearing wouldn't be appreciated.

'Mollie!' Margot yelled in the distance. 'Come and take a look at this.'

Scanning the many stalls in search of her sister, Mollie finally spotted Margot's blonde waves at yet another trinket stall.

'Has she always been like this?' Jasper groaned, struggling not to drop his growing collection of bags as he followed Mollie over to where Margot was standing.

'Like what?' Mollie replied. 'A magpie?'

'What was that?' Margot asked, narrowing her eyes at Mollie accusingly.

'We were just saying how lovely you are.' Smiling sweetly, Mollie linked her arm through her sister's. 'Isn't that right, Jasper?'

'Something like that.' Spotting Max at the doughnut stall, Jasper made his escape before Margot could laden him with yet more bags.

Too busy tossing items into her wicker basket to notice that her boyfriend had fled the scene, Margot pointed to a tiny gold tiara.

'Do you think Mum would like this?' She asked, motioning to the velvet-lined wooden box. 'I've been contemplating it for the last fifteen minutes.'

Puckering her lips, Mollie picked up the glistening tiara and turned it over in her hands.

'Something about it just screams *Mum*.' Tossing her icy blonde hair over her shoulder, Margot scratched the tip of her nose with a perfectly manicured nail. 'Do you know what I mean?'

The rows of twinkling stones dazzled under the bright string of fairy lights that dangled overhead, causing Mollie to blink repeatedly as she inspected the stamp on the gold band.

'Is this...'

'Nine-carat gold.' The voluptuous seller replied, ferociously chewing a piece of gum.

'And are these...'

'Several carats worth of cubic zirconia.' Looking rather pleased with herself, the seller shared a huge grin with Margot. 'Exquisite, isn't it?'

'It's beautiful.' Margot gushed, clutching her gloved hands to her cheeks. 'What do you think, Mollie?'

Still staring at the vulgar piece of jewellery, Mollie pursed her lips and remained silent.

'It's... different.' She eventually managed, choosing her words carefully as to not offend the vendor. 'It's a little on the small side.'

Throwing her head back, the seller let out a laugh that made the table shake.

'It's for a *baby*.' She explained, placing a rather patronising hand on Mollie's arm. 'It says so right there on the label.'

Slowly lowering her gaze to the wooden presentation box, Mollie ran her fingers over the velvet lining, which was more opulent than you would find in most coffins. Gulping at the obscene price tag, she ignored the impulse to ask what in the world a baby would want with a zircon-encrusted tiara.

'Take your time. It's a considered purchase, but that's the very last one.' Leaving Margot with the tiara, the vendor began to walk away. 'Today's my last day here. I won't be back until next year...'

'I'll take it!' Margot said hurriedly, causing the seller to stop in her tracks.

'She'll *think* about it.' Mollie corrected.

Feeling the seller's eyes burning into her, Mollie turned to face her sister and lowered her voice to a hushed whisper.

'Are you crazy?' She hissed, looking at Margot as though she had completely lost her mind. 'You're not seriously going to buy that monstrosity, are you?'

Seemingly baffled by Mollie's negative reaction, Margot frowned and ran her acrylic nails over the tiara.

'I think it's beautiful.' She replied defensively. 'And more importantly, I think Mum will too.'

'Margot...' Mollie replied slowly, really worrying that her sister had lost all sense of rationale. 'Mum doesn't have a baby. Why the hell would she want a gold tiara for a three-month-old?'

'I'm not buying it for a bloody baby, Mollie. I'm buying it for her Beanie Babies collection.' Margot explained. 'Sorry, didn't I say that?'

'No, Margot, you did not.' Suddenly convinced that Margot's winter trip to Skye had frozen every one of her brain cells, Mollie shook her head in disbelief. 'This conversation just got a whole lot weirder.'

'Mum's always been weird.' Margot replied, studying the tiara closely. 'The fact that she's been collecting Beanie Babies for the past ten years is relatively tame for her.'

'The Beanie Babies thing is fine.' Mollie insisted. 'Loads of people collect Beanie Babies. It's the tiara thing that makes it weird.'

'What makes it weird is that she puts her favourite one in a glass presentation box to shield it from the elements.' Raising a perfectly arched eyebrow, Margot giggled and shrugged her shoulders. 'But hey, I like to collect shells, she likes to collect Beanie Babies. Who are we to judge?'

'Let me get this straight.' Mollie said, moving aside as an eager customer loaded up a basket with various pieces of junk. 'You are planning on buying Mum a gold tiara for her to put on whichever one of her Beanie Babies makes it to the glittering heights of the glass presentation box?'

A flash of doubt crossed Margot's face before she placed the tiara into her basket adamantly.

'Well, what do you buy for the woman who's got everything?' She demanded, diving into her patent handbag for her purse. 'What have *you* got her?'

'Paperclip earrings.' Mollie replied proudly.

'Paperclip earrings?' Margot scoffed. 'And you're seriously giving me a hard time over a piece of fine jewellery?'

'I made those earrings myself!' Suddenly feeling rather defensive over her DIY Christmas gift, Mollie flashed her older sister a glare. 'I think you will find they are a very thoughtful and considered gift.'

'As is this!' Margot fired back, handing the delighted seller a handful of crisp notes. 'Thank you very much.'

The two sisters fell into silence as Mollie quietly seethed. So far, nothing had given her more confidence in her decision to go ahead with her no-Christmas Christmas than a blinged-up tiara for a collection of Beanie Babies.

'So, what's next?' Mollie grumbled, rubbing her hands together for warmth. 'Platinum toilet brush? Ruby doorstop?'

'Very funny.' Accepting a paper bag from the seller, Margot pulled her tartan scarf over her chin and started walking in the direction Jasper disappeared in earlier. 'If you can't spoil your loved ones at Christmas, when can you?'

Not wanting to bang on like a stuck record, Mollie decided to keep her opinions on Margot's ludicrous new purchase to herself. She was a firm believer in one man's trash being another man's treasure, but she also believed that *some* things in life were just plain stupid...

Chapter Six

Smothering her cheeks in mashed avocado, Mollie stared at her reflection from the comfort of her bed and giggled at the alarmingly green woman who was looking back at her. After an evening of subjecting her skin to sub-zero conditions, a little pampering was exactly what the doctor ordered. Mollie's favourite sitcom was on the television, Elvis was snoozing by her feet, and Max was casually flipping through the local newspaper, but their peace and quiet was about to come to an end.

'Can you hear that?' Max asked, dropping his newspaper onto the floral quilt and furrowing his brow. 'Turn the television down.'

Following his instructions, Mollie reached over to the bedside table and grabbed the remote control. As the cosy bedroom fell into silence, Mollie cupped a hand around her ear in an attempt to hear anything other than Elvis breathing deeply.

'I can't hear anything.' Returning to applying her face mask, Mollie increased the volume on the television before wiping her hands on a towel. 'Is your tinnitus playing up again? I warned you about standing too close to those speakers at the Christmas market.'

'It's not my tinnitus, Mollie. I can definitely hear...' Max's voice came to an abrupt stop as he raised his hand to his ear. 'Wait! There it is again!'

Hitting the mute button, Mollie closed her eyes in a bid to pinpoint the noise.

'*I could have been someone...*'

'Oh, hang on. I definitely heard that.'

'*So could anyone...*'

Bringing her eyes up to meet Max's, Mollie nodded as the penny finally dropped.

'Mrs Heckles.' They said in unison.

Laughing to herself, Mollie threw back the duvet and grabbed her dressing gown from the back of the bedroom door.

'I'll deal with it.' She said, motioning for Max to return to his newspaper. 'It's my turn.'

Quickly stuffing her feet into her slippers, Mollie flicked on the landing light and made her way down the stairs. The sound of Mrs Heckles' croaky voice drifted into the hallway from the open letterbox as Mollie searched the bowl next to the door for the keys. Unable to locate them beneath the mountain of bric-a-brac that Max had dumped in there, she bent down and peered through the letterbox.

'Hello, Mrs Heckles.'

'*Argh!*' Mrs Heckles cried, jumping backwards as Mollie's green face appeared before her.

'It's a face mask.' Mollie explained, really hoping Mrs Heckles' screams of horror hadn't woken the rest of the neighbours.

'You nearly gave me a damn heart attack!' Cursing loudly, Mrs Heckles clutched her chest. 'I thought you had finally turned into the Grinch!'

'Very funny.' Mollie replied. 'Have you quite finished with the serenading?'

'I've only just started!' Mrs Heckles said animatedly. 'What do you want next? A little Cliff Richards? He's not my favourite, but anything that gets you out of this slump works for me.'

'Mrs Heckles, this is the third time this week that you have treated us to your delightful dulcet tones.' Mollie said, yawning into her sleeve. 'Do you think you could possibly call it a night?'

'If that was a jibe at my singing voice, I'll have you know that I could have been a huge star back in the day, but the touring life didn't sit well with me.' Ignoring Mollie's question entirely, Mrs Heckles sighed wistfully. 'Groupies, junk food, cigarettes and alcohol...'

Being very aware that Mrs Heckles consumed more alcohol than Mick Jagger, Mollie simply smiled as Mrs Heckles began to lose herself in what could have been.

'Mrs Heckles?' Mollie interrupted softly. 'It's after midnight.'

'And?' She demanded. 'Are you afraid you're going to turn into a pumpkin?'

Yawning yet again, Mollie laughed and shook her head.

'As much as I love you serenading us, some of us have to get up for work in the morning.'

'Fine, but I'll be back.' Reluctantly giving in, Mrs Heckles groaned as she straightened her back. 'Until I see some evidence of Christmas going on here, you can expect me back louder and merrier than ever before.'

'I don't doubt it.' Mollie replied, watching her neighbour shuffle away. 'Goodnight, Mrs Heckles.'

Finally allowing the letterbox to close, Mollie waited until she heard Mrs Heckles' own door clunk shut before retreating up the stairs.

'She's gone.' Mollie announced, not bothering to remove her dressing gown before climbing back into bed next to Max.

'Has she been on the rum again?' He asked, looking up from his newspaper.

'Nope.' Pulling the duvet over her legs, Mollie grabbed a magazine from the bedside table and flipped it open. 'Sherry is her poison of choice at this time of year.'

'Whatever it is, it's certainly given her confidence in her singing abilities.' Max chuckled. 'She's been crooning like a canary.'

Laughing in agreement, Mollie turned the page of her magazine and stopped when yet another noise caught her attention.

'What now?' She cried exasperatedly, frowning in frustration. 'Can you hear that?'

'No.' Max replied, a little too quickly to be convincing. 'I can't hear anything.'

Turning the television up, Max blushed guiltily when Mollie immediately turned it back down.

'How can you not hear that?' She asked. 'It sounds like it's coming from beneath the bed.'

'It will be Mrs Heckles again.' Max said hurriedly. 'You know what she's like. She won't give up without a fight.'

Abandoning her magazine, Mollie leaned over the bed and lifted the duvet.

'*Max!*' She shrieked, inhaling sharply as she spotted Elvis tearing what looked suspiciously like an advent calendar to pieces. 'What the hell is this?'

'What's what?' He replied meekly, refusing to look her in the eye.

'Well, either Elvis has been down to Sainsbury's and bought himself an advent calendar or you have some explaining to do.' Mollie pulled Max towards her so that he too was hanging his head over the side of the bed.

'I can explain.' Max mumbled, failing to grab the offending advent calendar before Mollie got to it.

'Have you had this all month?' Holding the calendar an inch from her face, Mollie gasped when she realised the majority of the windows had already been opened. 'Max, I am so disappointed in you!'

'Oh, come on. It's only a few chocolates.' He protested. 'And you wouldn't have even known about it if it wasn't for the pesky cat.'

'But I *am* disappointed!' Mollie insisted in dismay.

'Don't say that.' Max groaned, stuffing the evidence back under the bed. 'Being disappointed is worse than being mad.'

'It's the secrecy that is the cause of my disappointment.' Mollie replied haughtily. 'Why didn't you tell me that you wanted an advent calendar? I'm not the Christmas police. You don't have to go to the extremes of hiding Christmas paraphernalia beneath the bloody bed.'

'Are you kidding me?' Laughing sarcastically, Max lifted Elvis up to join them on the bed. 'You're not the Christmas police, Mollie. You're the Christmas *mafia*.'

'I am not!' She retorted, her face mask cracking due to her frowning so furiously. 'That's slander!'

'Last week, you removed a nacho from Kenny's plate every time he mentioned turkey.' Max said matter-of-factly. 'That was just cruel. You know how much Kenny doesn't like to share food. You hit him where it hurts.'

'You're making me sound like some kind of monster.' Mollie replied quietly, recalling the look of dismay on Kenny's face as his pile of nachos became increasingly smaller.

'In my defence, you do look like a monster with all that green stuff on your face.' Propping a pillow behind his head, Max returned to his newspaper. 'Isn't it about time you washed that off? You're starting to look like Mrs Heckles' elbow.'

'There's nothing wrong with being a wrinkly old lady, Max.' Mollie retorted. 'And there's nothing wrong with wanting an advent calendar.'

Plucking the advent calendar from beneath the bed, Mollie walked across the bedroom and placed it on the dressing table.

'Wow!' Max mused. 'The Grinch *does* have a heart.'

Pausing in the doorway, Mollie winked before continuing on her way to the bathroom.

'Well, Max, there's time for a Christmas miracle yet...'

Chapter Seven

'Question seven... *If you were born on Christmas Day, what would your star sign be?*'

Puckering her lips, Mollie twirled a lock of hair around her finger and left the others to discuss the first question that she actually knew the answer to. The Blue Fajita quiz was always one of the highlights of her week, and despite the fact that this week's quiz was entirely focused on Christmas, Mollie was enjoying it more than ever.

For the first time in the lead-up to the big day, Mollie was allowing herself to enjoy the festivities. She might have declined a complimentary snowball from the eager bartender, and there may have been a roaring groan from the other punters when she refused to sign up to Christmas karaoke, but Mollie had let her hair down just enough to feel part of the celebrations.

'In case any of you missed it, I shall repeat the question one more time before we take a short break.' The quizmaster rambled into the microphone. '*If you were born on Christmas Day, what would your star sign be?*'

'Taurus.' Kenny replied confidently, draping an arm around Eugenie's shoulders. 'I should know as it's also my sign. You mess with the bull, you get the horns.'

Sniggering at his own joke, Kenny took a swig from his bottle of beer and reached for the pen that was in the centre of the table.

'Kenny, your birthday is in March, so it can't possibly be Taurus.' Taking the pen from his chubby fingers, Eugenie pulled the entry form towards her. 'How many star signs do you think there are?'

'Four.' Kenny answered boldly. 'One for each season.'

A stunned silence fell over the table as the group exchanged amused glances.

'How can you have a law degree yet not know how many

star signs there are?' Max asked, shaking his head at Kenny in bewilderment. 'Where was that degree from? Neverland?'

'Hey, I know my own star sign. Why do I need to know anyone else's?' Kenny frowned and shrugged his shoulders nonchalantly. 'When would knowing whether someone is a ram or a crab ever be useful to me?'

'It would be useful right now.' Max chuckled. 'If you knew there were more than four star signs, we might actually have a chance of winning the Christmas hamper.'

'Well, if *you* knew...'

'Does anyone else want to take a guess?' Eugenie chipped in, attempting to take control of the conversation before Max and Kenny could hit one another with their handbags. 'Anyone?'

'I'm quite sure it's Aquarius.' Tim offered. 'But as M-Dog just said, there's a festive hamper riding on this and I'm not confident enough to go with it.'

'Come on, Mystic Meg.' Max said, giving Mollie's arm a nudge. 'Enlighten us.'

'I must have been through the zodiac with you all a million times!' She exclaimed, taking the pen from Eugenie and filling in the quiz sheet. 'It's Capricorn!'

'That's why we bring her!' Max said proudly. 'And to kill the Christmas spirit, of course.'

'Don't use the C-word!' Kenny hissed, wrapping an arm around his beloved nachos protectively.

'Guys, you really don't need to walk on eggshells around me.' Offering her group of friends a bright smile, Mollie pulled her drink towards her. 'You *can* talk about Christmas.'

Desperate for her mission to remove the materialistic aspect from the festivities not to be misconstrued as her being the biggest humbug in town, Mollie cleared her throat and used her most sparkling tone of voice.

'Seriously, I am not the Ebenezer of Fulham!' She continued, attempting a friendly laugh. 'So, come on, tell me about your Christmas plans.'

A series of puzzled expressions stared back at Mollie before Tim broke the spell.

'Mollie, we're all coming to you for Christmas.' He said

slowly. 'Remember?'

'All?' She repeated, automatically looking at Eugenie and Kenny.

'That's still alright, isn't it?' Eugenie asked, her Hollywood smile faltering slightly. 'You did say that everyone was welcome.'

'Of course it's alright! The more the merrier!' Genuinely overjoyed that her friends had decided to spend Christmas with her, Mollie sat up straight and grinned widely. 'I'm just surprised, that's all. I seem to recall Kenny recoiling in horror when I invited you to join us?'

Quickly dismissing Mollie's claims, Eugenie shook her head and prodded Kenny in the ribs.

'That wasn't horror, Mollie.' Kenny said, rather unconvincingly. 'It was speechless joy. It's not my fault that I'm a hard man to read.'

Not being convinced by Kenny's feeble response, Mollie narrowed her eyes warily at a squirming Eugenie.

'Why the change of heart?' She asked, shifting her gaze from Kenny to Eugenie and back again. 'What's going on?'

Eugenie brushed her chocolate bob out of her face and took a deep breath before speaking.

'Okay...' She said, resting her elbows on the table. 'I must confess that it took a lot of bribery on my behalf, but I am pleased to say that I have *finally* managed to talk Kenny into taking you up on your very kind offer.'

'A lot of bribery.' Mollie repeated, raising her beer bottle to her lips. 'You make it sound like an invite to the morgue.'

'Sorry!' Looking completely mortified, Eugenie covered her eyes with her hands. 'That came out all wrong.'

'Did it?' Kenny asked, much to Eugenie's annoyance.

Choosing to ignore him, Eugenie reached across the table and placed a hand on Mollie's forearm.

'I think what you are doing is amazing.' She gushed. 'But Kenny here took a little more convincing. His belief that Christmas should be filled with endless expensive gadgets and more food than would be needed to feed every animal in London Zoo made me realise that *your* version of Christmas is exactly what he needed.'

Firing a glare in Kenny's direction, Eugenie rolled her emerald eyes.

'Now that he's come around to the idea that things will be a little different this year, he's really looking forward to it. Aren't you, Ken Ben?'

Muttering something beneath his breath, Kenny yelped when Eugenie kicked him beneath the table.

'I can't wait.' He said, scratching his newly implanted hair. 'We're really excited to experience Christmas in a way that opens our minds and souls to what is really important.'

'Did Eugenie tell you to say that?' Mollie asked in amusement.

'Yes.' Kenny admitted, causing Eugenie to deliver him a second swift kick.

'*Anyway...*' Giving Kenny yet another deathly stare, Eugenie turned back to Mollie. 'I have something that may be of interest to you.'

Reaching into her bag, Eugenie produced a glossy leaflet and slid it across the driftwood table.

'It's a scheme that has been implemented by a local charity to help people in the community over the festive period.' Eugenie explained happily. 'There are so many ways in which we can get involved. I thought this would fit in well with the message you are trying to get across.'

'What a great idea!' Mollie ran her eyes over the leaflet before passing it to Max. 'How do we sign up?'

'We should really have signed up at the start of December, but there's still time for us to get involved.' Crossing her long legs, Eugenie peeled the label off her beer bottle and tore it into tiny pieces. 'All you have to do is fill in a form on the website and they get back to you with a list of suitable activities. It's super easy.'

'I'm hearing a lot of *we* and *us* being thrown around in this conversation.' Tim said cautiously. 'I'm hoping that's just an innocent slip of the tongue?'

'Tim!' Mollie cried. 'You are going to sign up, aren't you?'

'I don't know, Molls.' Sharing uneasy looks with Max and Kenny, Tim shrugged his shoulders. 'I've already committed to your alternative Christmas. This might be a step too far, even for me.'

'Oh, come on!' Mollie persisted. 'This is a great opportunity to give something back to the community. We should all be getting involved with this.'

The silence that came back at Mollie was deafening as she looked at the many unimpressed faces around the table.

'Max, you're going to do this, right?' She asked, placing a hand on his thigh. 'Right?'

'*I'll* volunteer if *you* let us have a Christmas tree.' He offered, not missing a beat. 'How about that?'

'Absolutely not.' She fired back. 'You know I'm not doing traditions this year.'

'Those are my terms.' Max said smugly. 'Take it or leave it.'

Pulling her brow into a frown, Mollie lowered her gaze to the leaflet on the table. With her attempts at persuading people to rediscover the true meaning of Christmas proving fruitless, she quickly decided to put her time where her mouth was and her words into actions.

'A two-foot tree under the stairs.' She said firmly, holding out her hand to seal the deal. 'No baubles.'

'A six-foot tree in the window.' He countered. 'With lights.'

'A four-foot tree in the kitchen.' Positioning her hand inches from his, Mollie encouraged Max to shake it. '*No* lights.'

'I'm afraid that just doesn't work for me.' He said reluctantly, returning to his beer. 'Try again.'

Taking a deep breath, Mollie gritted her teeth and came back with her final deal.

'A five-foot tree in the living room. Just white lights.'

Max stared into the distance and considered Mollie's offer before speaking.

'Multicoloured lights, in the dining room...'

'My last offer or nothing!' Mollie interrupted. 'Deal or no deal?'

'Deal.' Max replied, shaking Mollie's hand before she could change her mind. 'Get in! We have secured a Christmas tree! This is not a drill!'

As Max and Kenny clinked their bottles together in celebration, Mollie sighed and turned her focus to Tim.

'Alright, Slease. What's it going to take for you to get

involved?' She asked, pushing the leaflet towards him. 'Hit me with it.'

'I'm going with a turkey.' Sliding the charity leaflet back to Mollie, Tim attempted to maintain his stern expression. 'You put a turkey on the table and you can me sign me up right here, right now.'

'A turkey?' She protested meekly. 'I'm already doing your beans and mash.'

'And I appreciate it, but an actual turkey to go with it would be the berries on my mistletoe.' Rolling up his sleeves, Tim reached for one of Kenny's nachos and scowled when he batted his hand away.

'I have to tell you, it's quite crude to bargain over charity work.' Mollie grumbled. 'The meaning of Christmas is to give up one's self and think only of others.'

'If it makes you feel any better, I've already signed up.' Eugenie whispered, putting the nachos out of Kenny's reach. 'Turkey or no turkey.'

'It would take more than a turkey for me to sign up.' Brushing nacho crumbs off his tie, Kenny rested his hands behind his head. 'A *lot* more.'

'Out of interest, what *would* it take?' Mollie asked, allowing her curiosity to get the better of her.

Tapping his fingers against his lips, Kenny stared into his beer as he chewed over Mollie's question.

'Trimmings.' He announced, licking his lips as the word tumbled out of his mouth. '*All* the trimmings.'

'Trimmings?' Mollie repeated. 'As in...'

'As in roast potatoes, pigs in blankets, stuffing, Brussels sprouts, parsnips, gravy...'

'I get the picture.' Mollie interjected, throwing Kenny a napkin before he could start drooling. 'Just to be clear, if Max gets a Christmas tree, Tim a turkey and Kenny all the trimmings he could possibly dream of, will you all sign up to the programme?'

An emphatic *yes* rang out around the table as Mollie held her bottle in the air.

'Fine.' Looking down at the charity leaflet, Mollie smiled as it twinkled back at her under the bright lights. 'So, do we have a deal?'

Chapter Eight

The quiz ended over an hour ago, but Mollie and the gang were only just leaving. Despite it being a school night, Kenny refused to leave the Blue Fajita until the rest of the bar had been subjected to his rather frightening renditions of every Christmas song ever recorded. Thankfully for the other customers, Eugenie finally managed to tear a hyper Kenny away from the microphone and declared it time for home.

Waving goodbye to the others, Mollie fished her gloves out of the depths of her handbag and waited for Max to zip up his coat.

'Are you sure you want to walk home?' He asked, tugging his woolly hat over his ears. 'We could take the Tube with the others?'

Shaking her head, Mollie looked up at the dark sky and smiled.

'It's such a beautiful night.' She said, holding out her gloved hands as a stream of snowflakes floated into her palm and immediately melted. 'Let's not waste it.'

'Walking it is.' Reaching into his pocket, Max pulled out an Ultimate Umbrella Cocoon and passed it to Mollie. 'Here, take this.'

'Would you mind if we went without the cocoons tonight?' Mollie asked, stepping aside as a young couple gently brushed past them on their way into the Blue Fajita. 'I want to feel the snow on my skin.'

Nodding in agreement, Max entwined his fingers with Mollie's as they began the long walk home. When the gang arrived at the Blue Fajita earlier, the streets were littered with animated revellers and frantic shoppers. Fast-forward a few hours and it would appear that the majority of people had taken shelter from the cold in the many restaurants that lined the pavement.

'Hey, do you remember when we first met and would spend

hours trying to spot shapes in the clouds?' Max asked suddenly.

Mollie smiled at the memory and nodded.

'Of course I remember.' She replied. 'Why do you ask?'

'No reason.' Inhaling deeply, Max blew a stream of breath into the air. 'What do you see in this?'

Squinting at the puff of condensation in front of them, Mollie was given three seconds to come up with an answer before it disappeared completely.

'Aunt Jacqueline?'

'You think *everything* looks like your aunt Jacqueline!' Max laughed and draped an arm around Mollie's shoulders. 'You said that weird piece of ginger we found at the supermarket looked like her.'

'That did look like her!' Mollie protested. 'The resemblance was uncanny.'

'I'm sure she would be thrilled to hear that.' Max replied, looking both ways before they crossed the dark street. 'But I suppose it's a step up from a shrivelled radish, which you have also compared her to in the past.'

Recalling the unfortunate-looking vegetable that arrived in their Ocado delivery, Mollie looked up at the twinkling Christmas lights overhead and inhaled the cold air. The many strings of colourful bulbs swayed in the breeze, casting a cosy glow over the falling snowflakes and everyone who walked amongst them.

'It looks like we're going to have a white Christmas.' Max mused, pulling Mollie closer as they turned the corner and headed down a residential side street. 'Just look at this. It wouldn't look out of place on a Christmas card.'

Taking a moment to admire the beautiful scene before her, Mollie fixed her focus on a particular house on her right. The blue door was showcasing a stunning wreath, which was dazzling brightly at passers-by. An enormous tree stood in the window, dressed exclusively in rich shades of red and gold. Behind the Christmas tree was a couple of young children. Wearing matching pyjamas and identical smiles, the two boys took it in turns to climb onto their father's shoulders and steal chocolate decorations from the tree.

Slowing down her pace, Mollie peered into the adjacent window and smiled at the sight of a frazzled-looking woman holding a glass of wine in one hand and a roll of wrapping paper in the other. Between taking sips from the glass, the weary woman attacked the huge pile of boxes in front of her with a determination Mollie had only seen before in aggressive shoppers at the Boxing Day sales.

'What do you think is in the boxes?' Mollie asked, finally tearing her eyes away from the window as they continued on their way.

'I think the beauty is in not knowing.' Max whispered. 'But if you're going to push me for an answer, I'm going to go with a delightful collection of tampon air fresheners.'

'Very funny.' A laugh escaped Mollie's lips as she batted Max's arm playfully.

The snow suddenly became heavier as they continued the journey home, causing a thick layer of sleet to dust the cold pavement ahead.

'It's really coming down now, isn't it?' Mollie remarked, bending down to scoop up a small mound of snow and allowing it to fall through her fingers. 'If this sticks, we might be able to make snow angels in the morning.'

'I haven't made snow angels since I was a boy.' Mimicking Mollie, Max picked up a handful of snow and grinned mischievously. 'Let's make them now!'

'We can't make them now, Max.' Mollie replied, jumping out of the way when Max threw a tiny snowball at her.

'Why?' He demanded.

'Because... because...'

As Mollie struggled to come up with a valid reason to dissuade him, Max ran over to a patch of pavement that hadn't yet been walked on and threw himself down to the ground.

'Max!' Mollie exclaimed, covering her mouth with her hand. 'Get up!'

'What was it that Dottie taught you?' He asked. 'Never put off until tomorrow what you can do today?'

Biting her lip, Mollie smiled sadly as she was reminded of Tim's mother's final pearls of wisdom.

'Well?' Max persisted. 'What are you waiting for?'

After having a quick glance around to make sure no one was looking, Mollie abandoned her inhibitions and lay down next to Max. Swinging her arms and legs in unison, she squealed as a patch of snow touched the back of her neck. With snowflakes landing on her face and the sound of Max's laughter ringing out around her, Mollie felt as carefree as she did when she was a child. The only difference being that the young Mollie who made snow angels in her grandparents' lawn had more than a mere centimetre of snow to work with.

As Max and Mollie wore the freshly fallen snow down to the concrete pavement, a light behind them caught Mollie's attention.

'Erm, Max?' She said, slowly pushing herself up. 'I think we should make a move.'

'Why?'

'Because I think we're on someone's driveway.'

Cocking her head towards the light, Mollie cautiously waved at the bewildered couple who were staring at them from their bedroom window.

'Oh...'

Hurriedly standing up, Mollie held out a hand to help Max to his feet before they made their escape into the night. The pair of them ran until their lungs burned, only stopping for breath when they reached the corner of their street. Holding on to a street light while she regained her composure, Mollie gasped for breath as Max pointed up at the sky.

'Mollie...' He panted, resting his hands on his knees. 'Look up.'

Shielding her eyes from the falling snow, Mollie squinted and took a step backwards.

'Is that...'

Before she could finish her sentence, Max pulled her towards him and planted a kiss on her lips. Mollie's cold nose pressed against Max's cheek as she wrapped her arms around him before pulling away.

'A kiss beneath the mistletoe.' Max remarked happily. 'Another of my Christmas wishes come true.'

Brushing her hair out of her face, Mollie scooped up a handful of snow and tossed it in his direction.

'If kisses were snowflakes, Max, I'd send you a blizzard...'

Chapter Nine

'Tim, you need to move faster!' Mollie hissed, clutching the base of the tree and scurrying towards the Payne and Carter office. 'Mrs Heckles moves faster than you and she's pushing ninety!'

'I'm trying, Molls, but it's not that easy to navigate.' Attempting to quicken his pace, Tim succeeded only in bumping into a suited man, who promptly gave him a furious glare. 'There's a reason they charge so much to deliver these things. Maybe you should have just paid the fee.'

Sticking to her guns, Mollie powered on through the crowds. To honour her part of the deal she struck with Max at the Blue Fajita last night, Mollie had spent her lunch hour scouring the shops for a five-foot Christmas tree. Not wanting to spend more than was absolutely necessary, she successfully talked the manager of the department store into selling the display tree to her for a fraction of the cost.

Albeit being minus its box, the manager regrettably declared that the cost of delivery would remain the same. Refusing to pay more for delivery than the price of the tree itself, Mollie quickly decided that she would deliver the tree by hand. With the help of Tim and a little elbow grease, she had managed to semi-successfully cart said tree through the busy streets of London.

'*Wait!*' Mollie shouted, causing Tim to come to an abrupt stop in the middle of the pavement. 'I need to check that the coast is clear before we approach the office. If James or Austin catch me with this, they'll probably fire me.'

Not waiting for a response, Mollie passed the entire weight of the tree to Tim and prowled towards the Payne and Carter building. Apart from Joyce, who was busy reading the obituaries in the newspaper, the foyer was completely empty, giving Mollie a perfect chance to sneak the tree into the building without being noticed.

'All systems are go!' Mollie whispered, waving her arms above her head to get Tim's attention. '*Go! Go! Go!*'

Right on cue, Tim hustled the tree between the sea of bewildered shoppers.

'Sorry!' He stammered, struggling to see where he was going as he fought against the many branches. 'Oops! Excuse me...'

Considering it was artificial, the Christmas tree Mollie had wangled was incredibly realistic. From the carefully crafted pine needles to the potted base, without close inspection, Mollie would have challenged anyone to prove it wasn't the real deal.

'Tim, watch out for the...' Mollie covered her eyes with her hands as Tim battled past a post box and knocked a branch off the Christmas tree in the process.

'What was that?' He asked, dropping the tree in front of Mollie and straightening yet another branch that had taken an almighty whack.

Knowing there was only a matter of seconds to spare before the foyer filled up with hungry employees in search of lunch, Mollie pulled Tim towards her.

'Here's what we're going to do.' Mollie said hurriedly, taking a second glance at an oblivious Joyce. 'I'm going to go inside and call the lift. Once it arrives, I'll give you the signal and you bring in the tree. We don't have much time, so we have to move quickly. Okay?'

Looking like a rabbit caught in the headlights, Tim nodded his head to show that he understood his role in the mission that lay ahead.

'Wait a minute!' He yelped suddenly. 'What's the signal?'

'The what?' Pausing with her hand on the door, Mollie frowned in confusion.

'The signal!' Tim replied, sounding incredibly flustered. 'The signal that tells me when it's time to bring the tree in!'

'Oh.' Biting her lip, Mollie offered Tim the thumbs-up sign. 'How's that?'

'Will you be using the left hand or the right?' He asked seriously.

'I don't know!' Starting to get impatient, Mollie shrugged

her shoulders. 'The left?'

'*Your* left, or *my* left as I look at you?'

Mollie responded with a glare that caused Tim to gulp loudly as he nodded his head.

'Either hand is fine.' He mumbled. 'Got it.'

Taking this as her cue to put their plan into action, Mollie slipped into the building and crept across the quiet foyer. Ensuring to keep the heels of her shoes off the tiled floor, she made it to the lift without Joyce being alerted to her presence. Luckily for Mollie, the doors to the lift opened the very second she pressed the button. Quickly jumping inside, she held the door open with her foot and gave Tim the all-important sign.

Immediately springing into action, Tim picked up the base and used his backside to push open the door to the building. No sooner had he stepped inside the foyer, Joyce folded the newspaper and pushed out her chair. Cursing beneath her breath, Mollie shooed Tim away and tried to think on her feet.

Just as she was about to abandon ship, Mollie was gifted with a light-bulb moment. Quickly grabbing her mobile phone out of her pocket, she dialled the Payne and Carter main switchboard. The sound of the phone ringing filled the empty reception area as Mollie watched Joyce yawn lazily before picking up the phone.

'Payne and Carter. Joyce speaking. How may I help you?'

Pinching her nose, Mollie attempted to make her voice as high as possible.

'Hello. This is Susannah Green from the Parakeet Pizza Company. I had a meeting with James Payne earlier today and I believe I may have left my... my haemorrhoid medication there. Could you possibly check the lost-and-found?'

'One moment.' Joyce grumbled gloomily. 'Please hold the line.'

'Thank you.'

Not being surprised that Joyce wouldn't question the validity of the rather anal Susannah Green requiring haemorrhoid medication, Mollie held her breath when Joyce disappeared behind the screen. Swiftly ending the call, she waved Tim inside and laughed as he clumsily raced across the reception floor as fast as his legs would carry him. Enjoying the sight of her friend fighting against the tree, Mollie decided not to tell him that it would take the particularly sedentary Joyce a good five minutes to walk to the lost-and-found, which happened to be little over ten feet away from her desk.

Coming to a stop at the lift, Tim frowned when he realised that the Christmas tree wasn't going to fit through the door without a fight. Mollie's tree might only have been five-feet tall, but it was also a good four-feet wide, hence the predicament they found themselves in.

'Molls, I don't think it's going to...'

'I got that, Slease.' Mollie grumbled, rubbing her temples wearily.

Hearing footsteps in the distance, Mollie quickly grabbed a branch and attempted to pull the tree towards her.

'Push it in, Tim!' She hissed. 'Go on! Just shove it! Give it some welly!'

After a few failed pushes, Tim took a step backwards and ran at the tree with all his might. Before she could shield herself from the impact, Mollie was knocked to the floor as the tree collapsed on top of her.

'We did it!' Tim cheered, joining Mollie in the lift and holding his hand up for a high five. 'Mission accomplished!'

'Not quite...' Struggling to her feet, Mollie slapped her hand against Tim's palm before pressing the button for his floor. 'We still need to take it to the IT department.'

'Yes.' Tim replied. 'Sorry, did you just say *IT department?*'

'I thought we could leave it in the storeroom until the end of the day.' Avoiding all eye contact, Mollie pretended to be engrossed in straightening the branches.

'I don't know about that, Molls.' Tim said uneasily. 'You know what Arnold is like.'

'It will be fine!' Mollie insisted, giving Tim her best reassuring smile. 'Nobody goes in that storeroom but you two. I'm sure you can keep him out of it until the end of the day.'

'Fine.' Tim reluctantly conceded. 'I'll do my best, but I can't promise anything. Arnold likes the IT department to be completely free of any religious or cultural influences. I accidentally left an Easter egg on my desk last year and he reported me to HR.'

Rolling her eyes, Mollie crossed her fingers in the hope that the lift wasn't going to stop before it reached Tim's floor.

'Are we also getting the turkey today?' Tim asked, rolling up his sleeve to study his watch. 'We have twenty-two minutes before the end of lunch, so there's still time.'

'Turkey?' Mollie repeated. 'What are you talking about?'

'The turkey.' Tim said slowly. 'That was the deal, right? Christmas tree for Max, turkey for me, trimmings for Uncle Ben. Eugenie has already signed us all up to the volunteer programme, so you have to keep your side of the bargain.'

'Don't worry, Slease.' Mollie replied. 'You will get your turkey, just not today. There's still a week to go until Christmas Day. Ideally, a turkey should only be kept for a couple of days before cooking.'

'I beg to differ, Molls. I beg to differ.' Checking his reflection in the mirror, Tim leaned against the railing as the lift continued to move. 'Mum used to buy her turkeys in the January sales. It's a huge saving! They pretty much give them away after Christmas.'

'You can buy turkeys in the January sales?' Mollie asked in disbelief. 'Really?'

'You can indeed.' Tim confirmed. 'The bottom drawer of the freezer was always reserved for Mum's turkeys.'

'You learn something new every day.' Mollie mumbled, brushing a smattering of artificial pine needles off her trousers.

'There was one year when she bought four of them.' Tim continued. 'Four years without having to fork out for a bird. Pure genius. The third Christmas was passable, but the fourth year was a bit of a disaster. Four years in the freezer reduced that last turkey to nothing more than a knackered old chicken. It was like chewing a boot.'

Physically shuddering, Mollie grabbed hold of the tree as the lift finally came to a stop.

'Thanks for that delightful description, Tim, but I think I'll stick with a fresh turkey if it's all the same with you?'

'It makes no difference to me, Molls.' Following Mollie out of the lift, Tim clapped her on the back and held open the door to the IT department. 'If I can stomach Mum's four-year-old bird, I can handle absolutely anything...'

Chapter Ten

Looking at Max's blank face, Mollie beamed brightly as she waited to hear the crucial verdict. The deafening silence in the living room made Max's feelings towards Mollie's offering quite clear, but in true Mollie style she refused to be anything but glowingly positive. After spending an afternoon in the IT storeroom and surviving a trip on the Tube, it was fair to say that Mollie's Christmas tree wasn't looking its best. Minus half of its original branches and suffering the addition of a rather large crack in the base, it certainly appeared worse for wear.

'A deal's a deal, Max.' Mollie said, attempting to straighten a branch and wincing when it fell onto the carpet. 'One five-foot Christmas tree.'

'I agree, Mollie. A deal's a deal.' Studying the tree carefully, Max cocked his head to the right. 'It's just...'

'Just what?' Mollie asked innocently. 'It's definitely five feet tall. I had the manager in the store measure it.'

'I think we both know that the height is not the problem here.' Max retorted. 'This thing looks like it went through a damn shredder.'

'Don't be so cruel, Max. All Christmas trees are beautiful.' Glossing over Max's fair criticism, Mollie dragged the bedraggled tree into the centre of the living room. 'This one has character, that's all. It's been a long, hard road to get him here.'

'A long, hard road?' Max repeated in amusement. 'That's a new way to describe the postal service.'

'Oh, this tree wasn't delivered.' Mollie replied, resting her hands on her hips. 'This tree has been carried through the heart of London, wedged into the IT storeroom *and* lived through a frankly horrifying journey on the Tube home. It's a miracle he is here to tell the tale.'

'Are you saying that you transported this thing home by yourself?' Max asked sceptically. 'Seriously?'

'I had a little help from my friends.' Deciding not to mention that good old Frankie picked her up from the Tube station and crammed the tree onto the back seats of his car, Mollie picked up the box of decorations that she pulled down from the loft earlier. 'If I remember correctly, the deal was a five-foot tree with lights.'

'That's correct.' Max confirmed, dropping down to his knees and rooting through the cardboard box. 'But I dread to think what you're going to pass off as *lights*.'

'What's that supposed to mean?' Mollie asked.

'Considering the state this tree is in, I wouldn't be surprised if you tied a few cotton balls to a shoelace and tried to convince me it brings a certain *charm* to the tree.'

Laughing along, Mollie took a seat next to him and turned up the fire.

'You didn't pay for this thing, did you?' Max asked, giving the tree another dubious glance as Elvis wandered into the room to join them. 'If you admit to dragging it out of a skip, I won't judge you.'

'For the last time, Max, it didn't look like this in the shop!' Mollie retorted exasperatedly. 'But if it makes you feel any better, it was half-price.'

'That does make me feel a little better, but I do believe I'm entitled to a little reimbursement for receiving such damaged goods.' He said seriously, pushing the box of glistening decorations towards Mollie. 'For every broken branch, I am happy to accept a bauble by way of compensation.'

'Compensation?' Mollie repeated, trying to fight her growing grin. 'Are we really going to haggle over Christmas decorations?'

'We most certainly are.' Shooting Mollie a playful smile, Max plucked a gold bauble from the box. 'One bauble, one branch. Do we have a deal?'

Being very aware that every court in the country would rule in favour of Max deserving some recompense for his rather pitiful excuse for a tree, Mollie decided not to negotiate and agreed to his offer.

'Deal.' She said, offering her hand to make it official. 'But I get to decide which baubles.'

'I'm not going to argue with that.' Shaking Mollie's hand, Max pushed himself up. 'You choose the baubles while I pour us a couple of drinks.'

As Max went to prepare refreshments, Mollie crawled around the tree and quickly counted the damaged branches. Upon giving the tree a close inspection, she decided that Max was quite right to be disappointed. The tough journey home had made the once beautiful tree look rather tattered indeed. It would be more suited to a Halloween party than a Christmas celebration.

Returning to the box of decorations, Mollie reached into the stash and pulled out a glass bauble. After quickly polishing it on her sleeve, she held it up to the light and smiled. When Mollie and Max got married, Tiffany and Ralph gifted them the intricate decoration and Mollie had cherished it ever since. A knotted piece of rope was encased inside the frosted globe, surrounded by copious amounts of white glitter. The gold loop was embossed with the date of their wedding in delicate lettering, simply adding to the beauty of the ornament. It wasn't like anything she had ever seen before. Nothing about it screamed Christmas, but it really struck a chord with Mollie.

Each year, when she slipped it onto a branch of the tree, Mollie would feel a sense of pride that she had been lucky enough to see another year through to the end. Tiffany always joked that if Mollie and Max ever divorced, they had to smash it on the ground and untie the rope, but despite a rather *ropey* period a short while back, the ornament was still in one piece.

Placing the bauble on the coffee table, Mollie returned to the box of decorations and chose a couple of gingerbread men, along with the gold star she bought in the John Lewis sale last January. Fingering the two turtle doves her grandmother gave her when she was a child, Mollie looked up when Max walked back into the room with two glasses in his hands.

'What constitutes a *broken* branch?' She asked, accepting a glass of red and looking at the pile of decorations she had chosen.

'Anything that has been damaged since leaving the shop.' He replied. 'If the mutilation happened after money was exchanged then I'm entitled to a bauble for it.'

Biting her lip, Mollie took a sip of wine and nodded as Max perched on the arm of the sofa to stroke Elvis.

'It must be so confusing for him to see a tree inside the house.' Max commented, smiling as Elvis playfully batted his hand. 'Remember when I designed that litter tray with the artificial foliage? He destroyed that thing within thirty seconds of setting eyes on it. Maybe I should devise some kind of security cage for the tree...'

As Max rambled about the many ways in which they could protect the Christmas decorations from their lethal kitten, Mollie lowered her gaze to the turtle doves that were still in her hand. Being very aware that she had already chosen more decorations than there were broken branches, she pursed her lips and sighed. Wandering around the tree, Mollie secretly snapped off another branch before adding the turtle doves to the heap of decorations on the coffee table.

'So, is this my recompense for the devastating destruction my tree endured?' Max joked, picking up the turtle doves and quickly moving them when Elvis took a predictable swipe. 'Wow! I forgot about these! I can't believe they're still in one piece. These things look older than I am.'

'That's because they are.' Working her way around the tree, Mollie made an attempt at fluffing up the branches. 'My grandmother was given them by her mother, so I can only imagine how old they actually are.'

'In that case, get them on there.' Max insisted, passing the turtle doves to Mollie. 'What are you waiting for?'

'The lights need to go on first.' Returning to the box, Mollie pulled out a string of tangled fairy lights. 'How the hell do these end up so knotted? Every year I put them away neatly, and every year I open the box to see a tangled web of bulbs.'

'Not exactly.' Max corrected. 'Every year you throw them into the box without a second thought, and every year you open said box and complain that *somehow* the lights have mysteriously tied themselves up in knots. Sound familiar?'

'Nope.' Mollie lied. 'Not at all.'

Chuckling to himself, Max placed his wine glass on the sideboard and walked over to the sound system.

'How do you feel about a little music?' He asked cautiously.

'Nothing too festive, just a little something to set the mood while we are decorating the tree.'

Before Max could say *Alexa*, Mollie shook her head.

'The deal was…'

'I know what the bloody deal was, Mollie!' Max cried, cutting her off mid-sentence. 'But can you forget about fighting traditions for a moment and just allow yourself to enjoy them if the mood takes?'

Concentrating on untangling the lights, Mollie soaked up Max's words like a sponge.

'Fighting them for the sake of fighting them is as bad as doing them for the sake of doing them.' He persisted, watching Elvis study the Christmas tree curiously. 'Mrs Heckles will be screeching through the letterbox soon, so we might as well listen to someone who can sing *without* rounding up the stray cats of the neighbourhood before she gets here.'

'Fine.' Mollie said. 'Just don't expect me to sing along.'

Finally removing a knot from the string of lights, she cheered and moved on to the next.

'Let's have some Michael Bublé, at least he won't bring feral cats to our door.' Max teased, instructing Alexa to play his favourite Christmas album before Mollie could change her mind.

'Give me those lights. We'll be here all night at this rate.'

As the stereo jumped into life, Mollie watched Max expertly untangle the wire in a matter of seconds.

'*Voila!*' He said. 'Make sure you leave the top branch free for the topper.'

Doing as he instructed, Mollie began weaving the fairy lights between the thin branches.

'It might help if you plugged them in.' She said, struggling to see what she was doing. 'I've got more chance of finding a shadow in the dark than I have of spreading these out evenly.'

'Good point.' Passing Mollie her glass of wine, Max plugged in the lights at the socket. 'I would offer to help, but we both know your perfectionism makes this more of an ordeal than an enjoyable festive activity.'

'Not this time.' Mollie replied, pushing the box of decorations towards him. 'This year, there are no rules whatsoever. Knock yourself out.'

Seemingly unconvinced, Max glanced at the box and took a swig of wine.

'Mollie, the last time I tried to help you decorate the tree, you nearly *did* knock me out.' He said seriously. 'I placed a red bauble too close to another red bauble and you threw the turtle doves at my head.'

'I didn't *throw them at your head*, Max.' Mollie retorted, her cheeks burning at the memory. 'I merely tossed them in your direction. It's not my fault you have the reflexes of a sleeping sloth.'

'Is that so?' A slight smile played on the corner of Max's lips as he wandered around the living room. 'What about the time that you toppled the entire tree over because I put the chocolate decorations next to the radiator?'

'Are you going to help me or not?' Mollie demanded. 'I'm only doing this for you, remember?'

'I'm going to help.' Picking up the box, Max began to search through the decorations. 'I'm just hoping my old fencing mask is in here.'

Mollie rolled her eyes and returned her attention to the tree.

'I'm kidding!' Laughing loudly, Max chose a bauble from Mollie's pre-selected pile. 'I'm just surprised by your casual approach to this, that's all. I have to be on my guard.'

Determined to prove Max wrong, Mollie simply smiled in response and continued to drape the lights around the tree. Too consumed with making sure they were perfectly distributed, Mollie almost didn't notice when Max clapped his hands together to indicate that he was done.

'You're not leaving them like that, are you?' She asked, pointing to the decorations that had been carelessly shoved onto the bottom row of branches.

'Yes.' Studying Mollie's face closely for a reaction, Max folded his arms in amusement. 'That's not a problem for you, is it?'

'Nope.' Pursing her lips, Mollie shook her head and inhaled sharply. 'It's just... lumping them all in one place like that makes the tree look slightly *unbalanced*.'

'Unbalanced?' Max repeated, clearly enjoying taunting

Mollie. 'And that's bad because...'

'Not *bad*. I never said *bad*.' Scratching the tip of her nose, Mollie slowly counted to ten. 'You simply have a certain artistic flair that I am obviously too narrow-minded to understand.'

'Artistic flair.' Max echoed proudly, tossing a bauble in the air. 'I have always fancied myself as the next Tracey Emin. I've never been one to follow the crowd.'

Wincing as Max caught the glass bauble seconds before it could smash into a million pieces, Mollie grabbed a bauble of her own and slipped it onto a bare branch. Taking great care to ensure the decoration wasn't obstructed by any lights or neighbouring branches, she smiled in satisfaction and plucked another from the coffee table.

As she lost herself in bringing the sorry-looking tree to life, Mollie completely forgot about her no-Christmas Christmas and sang along to the music under her breath. Without thinking, she moved on to the remaining decorations and continued to add touches of sparkle to the tree. Despite it being one of her favourite festive activities, Mollie had always believed that decorating a tree was simply a formality of the festivities. However, as she saw the bare tree come alive before her eyes, she felt a spark reignite inside her.

Smiling happily at the progress she had made, Mollie frowned when she realised that Max was staring at her intently.

'Why are you looking at me like that?' She asked, suddenly feeling self-conscious. 'What is it?'

'I just love seeing you like this.' Max replied. 'This is my favourite thing about Christmas.'

'Decorating the tree?' Mollie asked, reaching into the box of decorations.

'Not decorating the tree. Watching *you* decorate the tree.' Leaning against the wall, Max allowed Elvis to paw his socks. 'I love the way your nose screws up when you're paying such attention to detail. I love the way you chastise anyone who dares to help without the flair of Laurence Llewelyn-Bowen. And I love the way you make the room *feel* like Christmas. It's quite a talent you have.'

Feeling her lips stretch into a bashful smile, Mollie grinned at Max from the opposite side of the Christmas tree.

'Does it feel like Christmas now?' She asked, walking over to him and wrapping her arms around his waist.

Max stared at his messy attempt at dressing the tree and shook his head slowly.

'Not really.' He admitted. 'But I can't quite put my finger on why.'

Immediately recognising what the problem was, Mollie grabbed the base of the tree and turned it around.

'How about now?' She asked, placing her hands on her hips as she studied her immaculately presented side. 'Is that any better?'

'*Now* it feels like Christmas.' Smiling brightly, Max nodded and massaged Mollie's shoulders as they admired her handiwork. 'Look at it. It's perfect.'

'It's all about spacing.' Mollie explained. 'You have to ensure that each decoration is equidistant from the rest.'

'Is that so?' Max whispered, resting his chin on Mollie's head. 'I have to say, there seems to be a heck of a lot of decorations on there. What happened to one bauble, one branch?'

Taking the turtle doves from the coffee table, Mollie wiped a layer of dust off the top before slipping them onto the last remaining branch.

'On reflection, I think the damage was far more considerable than we originally thought.' She said, using her most serious tone of voice. 'With that in mind, it's only fair that you're compensated accordingly. Just look at this crack in the pot. Surely that demands a few pieces of tinsel?'

Covering his mouth with his hand, Max nodded sternly.

'I hate to agree with you, Mollie, but this level of destruction is definitely going to require an increase in compensation.' He said. 'I'm thinking tinsel, Christmas crackers and those hideous beads Mrs Heckles gave us. What are you thinking?'

'You know what, Max?' Mollie replied, smiling up at him. 'I think you're absolutely right...'

Chapter Eleven

Struggling to keep up with Eugenie as she dragged her through the frenzied shopping centre, Mollie clutched her handbag tightly and checked her watch. The usually busy complex was more hectic than ever, making the simple act of walking in a straight line almost impossible.

'How much further is it?' Mollie asked, looking over her shoulder to make sure they hadn't lost Tim in the swarms of people. 'I have to be back at the office in thirty minutes. I've told you before how particular James Payne is about punctuality.'

Not being deterred by Mollie's incessant wittering, Eugenie continued to march through the relentless shoppers regardless. Her refusal to tell them where they were heading was originally intriguing to Mollie and Tim, but as the minutes ticked by, they were becoming increasingly agitated at the thought of being late for work.

'Tim sets a timer on his phone to make sure he doesn't take a single minute more than he's allocated.' Mollie persisted, dodging a rather determined shopper. 'Don't you, Slease?'

'I sure do, Molls.' Finally catching up, Tim tossed a handful of coins into a collection box. 'And I can tell you that we have... *twenty-seven minutes and forty-three seconds* until we absolutely have to be back in the office.'

'Don't worry!' Eugenie said animatedly, easily weaving between the many eager punters. 'This won't take long. It's just around this corner.'

'You've said that three times already!' Mollie protested. 'Can't you just tell us what we are doing here?'

Shaking her head, Eugenie flashed Mollie an excited smile.

'All you need to know is that it will be worth it.' She said, picking up the pace. 'You just need to have a little patience.'

'We now have twenty-six minutes.' Tim announced, studying his phone carefully. 'It will take us a good eleven minutes to get back to the office, which means you have just fifteen minutes to show us whatever it is you want to show us. But if it's the cut-price turkey lasagne in the food court, I've already seen them and stocked the freezer to capacity.'

'I'm surprised you have any room left in your freezer after the two dozen sardine pies you bought when Iceworld closed down.' Mollie said, struggling to keep up with Eugenie's gazelle-like strides.

'You must be joking!' Tim chuckled. 'I polished those off within a week of buying them. Those pies were a treat for the senses.'

Grimacing at the thought of Tim devouring sardine pies like they were going out of fashion, Mollie raised a hand when she spotted Eugenie in the throngs of people up ahead.

'What is she pointing at?' Tim asked, straining his neck as he attempted to see what was causing Eugenie to grin so manically.

'I don't know.' Mollie replied. 'But it seems we're about to find out...'

Finally coming to a stop in front of Eugenie, Mollie and Tim turned to look in the direction of which she was gesturing. A quaint cavern covered in artificial snow stood before them. Huge candy canes formed a path through the glitter-drenched path, and a queue of eager children waited in line for their turn to enter.

'It's a grotto.' Mollie said in confusion. 'Have you brought us here to sit on Santa's lap?'

Squirming uncomfortably, Tim looked around for an escape route.

'I don't really like to talk about it, but I had a terrible ordeal in a grotto.' He revealed. 'Six-year-old Tim pulled on the beard, Santa swore and told young Timothy he would be getting socks for Christmas. I still haven't dealt with it until this very day, so I would rather sit this one out if it's all the same with you two.'

'Tim, we aren't actually going to sit on Santa's lap!' Mollie said, laughing as she turned to Eugenie. 'Are we?'

Shaking her head, Eugenie led them towards the grotto.

'What do you see?' She asked, positioning herself between

Mollie and Tim. 'Look closely.'

More confused than ever, Mollie shrugged and studied the scene in front of her.

'A grotto?' She said. 'Children, gifts, elves, snow...'

'Go back one.' Eugenie interrupted.

'Snow?'

'Back again.'

'Elves?'

'Bingo.' Eugenie whispered.

Pointing to a rather rotund elf who was keeping the queue of rowdy kids in line with a particularly grouchy expression on his face, Eugenie waited for the penny to drop.

'It's... it's...' Mollie stammered, covering her mouth with her hand as a shocked gasp escaped her lips.

'Uncle Ben.' Tim finished for her. 'It's Uncle Ben.'

Barking orders at the rowdy rabble, Kenny yanked a candy cane out of the ground and used it to bat the children away from the entrance. His pointed shoes, striped tights and floppy hat made him fit in perfectly with the rest of the elves, but the words that were pouring out of his mouth made it clear to anyone who was watching that this was a rather naughty elf indeed.

'Get back, you little rascals!' Kenny hollered, waving the candy cane around wildly. 'The next person who steps out of line has their presents sent to the chipper!'

The bells on his shoes jangled loudly as the gaggle of boisterous children took great delight in swinging from Kenny like a pack of raucous monkeys at feeding time.

'Quit messing around!' He yelled. 'You know the rules! Three strikes and you're out! Especially you with your finger up your nose!'

'I've got to get a picture of this.' Quickly whipping her phone out of her pocket, Mollie tapped on the camera and the flash lit up the grotto. 'Smile, Kenny!'

Finally looking up, Kenny abruptly dropped the candy cane when he realised Mollie, Tim and Eugenie were waving at him from across the shopping centre.

'That damn turkey better be worth this!' He shrieked, before yelping out loud when one of the older children jumped on his foot. 'Hey, you little...'

As Mollie and Tim promptly erupted into hysterics, Eugenie draped her arms around their shoulders.

'So...' She said. 'Was this worth giving up your lunch hour for?'

'Absolutely!' Still snapping away with her camera, Mollie wiped tears of laughter from her cheeks. 'I would give up my lunch breaks for the entire year to see this!'

'See!' Eugenie exclaimed happily, her eyes glistening. 'I told you this charity scheme would be fun!'

'Wait a minute.' Finally stopping laughing for long enough to process what Eugenie was saying, Tim frowned in confusion. 'This is for the volunteer programme we signed up to?'

'Of course it's for the volunteer programme!' Eugenie replied, exchanging tickled glances with Mollie. 'Do you think this is just how Kenny likes to spend his spare time?'

Shrugging his shoulders, Tim stuffed his hands into the pockets of his black mac.

'I'll have you know that Uncle Ben has been known to do some pretty wacky things in the name of fun.' Tim revealed. 'He once filled his bath with custard just to see if he could float.'

'Does it look like he's having fun to you?' Eugenie asked, deciding to breeze past the random custard story.

Looking over at the grotto, Tim shook his head when Kenny's squeals filled the air once more. Attempting to stop the many lawless children from throwing artificial snowballs at passing shoppers, the usually confident Kenny looked well and truly out of his depth.

'The kids are certainly having fun.' Mollie mused, linking her arm through Eugenie's and giggling. 'Forget Santa, I think Kenny is the star of this show.'

Tim laughed along as Kenny attempted to run away from the gang of children and tripped over his candy cane in the process. Mollie fully expected the volunteer work to be invaluable, but as she watched Kenny being bombarded with snowballs, she decided that the best things in life weren't just free, they were absolutely priceless.

Chapter Twelve

'Figs?' Mollie said, peering at Mrs Heckles over the edge of the notepad she was holding. 'You want *twelve* cans of tinned figs?'

'That's right.' Mrs Heckles confirmed confidently. 'Write it down, and don't buy the own brand ones. Those things look like the stuff the cat hacks up.'

Mollie looked down at Misty and smiled when she gave her tail a cursory swish before immediately falling back to sleep. For the last fifteen minutes, Mollie had been making a list of her neighbour's shopping requirements from the comfort of Mrs Heckles' festive living room, and as her notepad filled up with more random requests, Mollie was becoming increasingly confused.

The heat from the glowing fire was tempting Mollie to give in to her tired eyes and grab forty winks, but a poke from Mrs Heckles' walking stick made her jolt to attention.

'Whitening toothpaste.' Mrs Heckles demanded. 'The one from the advert. You know the one. The one where that pretty girl whitens and buggers off.'

'*More* whitening toothpaste?' Mollie asked, tapping her pen against the notepad. 'Are you sure?'

'Yes.' Casting a glare in Mollie's direction, Mrs Heckles tested the temperature of the radiator with her foot. 'Why is that comical to you?'

'It's not.' Mollie protested, quickly adding it to her list. 'If you want whitening toothpaste, you shall have it, but you have to be careful using those harsh whiteners on your veneers.'

'I'll decide how white my own teeth are, young lady.' Puckering her lips, Mrs Heckles tossed a mint imperial to Mollie. 'Put some of those on the list too.'

'You're the boss.' Turning the page, Mollie made a scribble

in the notepad and sat up straight. 'Is there anything else? It's going to drop below freezing for the next couple of days, so I don't really want you venturing outside.'

Rolling her eyes, Mrs Heckles muttered something under her breath and turned the volume up on the television.

'Just to be clear, that means no letterbox serenading.' Mollie said sternly. 'The last thing you want is to take a tumble and end up spending Christmas in the hospital.'

'At least I would get a proper Christmas dinner in the hospital.' Mrs Heckles retorted. 'Better still, I could climb onto the supermarket roof in a silly costume like that fool did last week and get myself thrown into jail for the night. I bet they get a half-decent meal in there too.'

Placing the notepad onto the bookcase next to her, Mollie pulled the crochet throw over her lap and smiled.

'Well, I am sure you will be very pleased to hear that you shall be getting a turkey dinner with all the trimmings after all.' Mollie announced smugly. 'How about that?'

Slowly turning to look at Mollie, Mrs Heckles widened her eyes.

'It's a Christmas miracle!' She whispered. 'It was my singing, wasn't it?'

'Actually, it was...'

'It was the damn carols and you know it!' Letting out a cackle that caused the many Christmas cards on the mantlepiece to quiver, Mrs Heckles picked up her doily and waved it around triumphantly.

'Your singing *might* have had a *little* bit of an impact.' Mollie admitted. 'But you ultimately have the Rainbow Volunteer Group to thank for answering your Christmas wishes.'

'Rainbow Volunteer Group?' Mrs Heckles repeated, dropping her doily onto the nest of tables.

'Eugenie found a flyer at the supermarket requesting volunteers and signed me up.' Mollie explained. 'It did take a bit of haggling to coax the rest of our group to do the same, hence the five-foot tree that's currently in my living room.'

'You got a tree too?' Mrs Heckles shrieked, her glasses sliding down the bridge of her nose. 'Blimey! Did you get a bump on the head?'

'Not unless you count the wind chime that hit me in the face on the way over here.' Rubbing her sore forehead, Mollie adjusted the throw to cover her cold feet. 'You really need to move that, Mrs Heckles. It's going to take someone's eye out.'

'I think you'll find that wind chime has been up there for fifteen years and it's never bothered me.' Wrapping her dressing gown tightly around her body, Mrs Heckles jutted out her chin defiantly. 'The wind chime stays where it is.'

Resisting the urge to tell Mrs Heckles that the reason said wind chime hadn't ever bothered her was that she wasn't more than four feet tall, Mollie decided to move the conversation along.

'Anyway...' She said, stifling a yawn. 'I think this volunteer group is a wonderful cause and I genuinely can't wait to get stuck in.'

'It's a fabulous cause.' Mrs Heckles agreed. 'Brenda has a visit from them every year.'

'She does?' Mollie asked, the realisation that Mrs Heckles was already aware of the group piquing her interest.

Mrs Heckles nodded and popped another mint imperial into her mouth.

'They do the rounds at Zumba Gold.' She explained, flicking through the television magazine. 'A lot of old dears from the retirement home on Fountain Street attend those classes. Most of them don't have any family left, so this time of year can be a bit hard for them.'

Mollie smiled sympathetically as Misty jumped onto her lap and immediately kneaded the throw.

'The Rainbow charity visits the retirement home in the run-up to Christmas and reads books to them over a pot of tea.' Mrs Heckles continued. 'It's a bit twee for me, but Brenda is always the first to get involved. With her family being in New Zealand, she welcomes any company that's on offer. They're reading A Christmas Carol at the moment, it's one of Brenda's favourites.'

'What is Brenda doing for Christmas?' Mollie asked, scratching Misty behind her ears while she purred wildly. 'She isn't spending it alone, is she?'

'In a fashion.' Sucking on her mint, Mrs Heckles removed her glasses and rubbed her eyes. 'She spends the entire day talking to her daughter on the internet. They watch each other open their presents, they cook their lunch together... they even have a glass of sherry to finish the night off. It's like they're right there in the room with her.'

'That's lovely.' Mollie replied. 'What a great use of the internet.'

'Oh, Brenda would be lost without the spider's web. She thinks it's the greatest invention since underwired bras...'

As Mrs Heckles filled Mollie in on all the mischief Brenda and her daughter got up to during their weekly Skype sessions, Mollie's mind drifted to her upcoming project with Tim. Their plans to bring Dottie Parents to life in memory of Tim's mother had been put on the back burner until the new year, but that hadn't stopped Mollie from making more plans than her brain could handle. As such, she often found herself drifting into a world of logo designs, website layouts and possible marketing campaigns at any given opportunity.

'So, what shall you be doing for the charity?' Mrs Heckles asked, popping Mollie's thought bubble. 'If you're going to be reading at the retirement home, stay away from Barney. He doesn't clean his dentures.'

'Actually, I don't know what I'll be doing.' Crossing her fingers that she didn't find herself donning an elf suit à la Kenny, Mollie let out another yawn. 'Eugenie has volunteered to be chief organiser and is keeping us all in the dark until Saturday. Hopefully, I'll find myself reading Charles Dickens to Brenda.'

'I wouldn't hold your breath.' Mrs Heckles scoffed. 'Brenda has had Connie read to her for the past two years. She wouldn't be very pleased if anyone else showed up. She might play the innocent, but Brenda can be a demon if she doesn't get her own way. She hit old Rupert over the head with a Christmas cracker last week after he refused to give her his paper hat. It caused quite a stir in the bingo hall. Security had to prise them apart.'

Deciding not to question why Mrs Heckles' bingo hall had a security guard, Mollie gently placed Misty on the floor and pushed herself up.

'On that note, I better be going.' She said, reaching for her coat. 'And remember, I won't be here tomorrow.'

Shrugging her shoulders in confusion, Mrs Heckles waited for Mollie to explain further.

'The office Christmas party?' Mollie said, slipping her hands into her pockets. 'It's tomorrow night.'

'Of course!' Shaking her head irritably, Mrs Heckles closed the television magazine and dropped it onto the floor. 'Don't get old, Mollie. It's a terrible thing.'

'Well, I think you pull off *old* rather well.' Mollie replied playfully. 'If I am half as fabulous as you are at your age I shall count myself very lucky.'

'Give over!' Brushing off Mollie's compliment, Mrs Heckles tried to hide her pink cheeks behind the collar of her dressing gown. 'Enjoy your party, and don't do anything I wouldn't do... or most of the things I would.'

Laughing along, Mollie tugged her handbag onto her shoulder and stroked Misty on the head.

'Enjoy your evening.' She said, discreetly taking the decanter from the coffee table and hiding it behind the bookcase. 'Go easy on the sherry.'

After giving her a quick hug, Mollie left Mrs Heckles to watch her beloved shopping channels and let herself out of the living room. Pausing in the hallway to ensure she had picked up her mobile phone, Mollie dived into her handbag and frowned when her fingers landed on a folded piece of paper.

Suddenly remembering that she had signed up for Secret Santa, Mollie groaned and slowly unravelled the crumpled strip. Her knee-jerk frustration melted away the second she saw the handwritten name in front of her. Dropping the strip of paper into her pocket before stepping out onto the cold street, Mollie felt her lips stretch into a smile as an idea came to her.

They say it's not the gift but the thought that counts, and for this particular person, Mollie knew *exactly* what gift to give.

Chapter Thirteen

Finally closing the folder in front of her, Mollie stretched out at her desk and rubbed her tired eyes. After studying marketing proposals for the past two hours she was in dire need of a rest, but if her mounting list of unanswered emails was anything to go by, Mollie had a while to go before she could succumb to some much-needed R and R. Fighting the growing urge to procrastinate, she raised her hand in acknowledgement when she spotted Joyce heading her way with a huge red sack trailing behind her.

With the office party due to start as soon as the clock ticked past five o'clock, Mollie had been wondering when she would have a visit from the world's gloomiest receptionist.

'Hello, Joyce.' She said, relieved to squeeze in a few moments of idle chit-chat before succumbing to her inbox. 'You look very snazzy today.'

'I picked this up at a charity shop back in the summer.' Dropping the sack next to Mollie's desk, Joyce brushed a stray piece of cotton off her sparkly blouse. 'It was only eight pounds and it still had its tag.'

'Wow.' Mollie replied, surprised to see Joyce smiling for once. 'What a bargain.'

Before she met Joyce, Mollie had never heard of CPD, but she was now in no doubt that Compulsive Price Disclosure existed. From confessing that her hair was permed free of charge by the local hairdressing college to revealing that her handbag was just three pounds at her favourite car boot sale, Joyce returned every compliment with a statement about the fabulously low price.

'I like a bargain.' Joyce said solemnly. 'It's so much more satisfying when things don't break the bank.'

'Don't we all.' Mollie replied, twirling her pen around her fingers. 'So, I'm guessing you're here to collect the Secret Santa gifts?'

'How did you know?' Joyce asked, her frown intensifying.

'Well, the big red sack might have been a slight clue.' Pushing back her seat, Mollie smiled and pulled open the filing cabinet next to her desk. 'It makes a change from your usual patent number.'

'That tote was four pounds from the flea market.' Joyce bragged. 'It was practically new too.'

Nodding in approval, Mollie rifled through the paperwork before pulling out a glittering envelope.

'There you go, Joyce.' Dropping the envelope into the sack, Mollie folded her arms. 'Will I be seeing you at the party later?'

'I'm counting down the hours as we speak.' Joyce mumbled. 'I can hardly contain myself.'

'Okay then.' Mollie replied, watching Joyce head for the lift. 'Don't you be going crazy now.'

Exhaling loudly, Mollie prepared herself to succumb to her mountain of waiting emails, but luckily for her James Payne had other ideas.

'Mollie?' James said, sticking his head out of his office and beckoning her towards him. 'I have a job for you.'

Responding with a firm nod of the head, Mollie locked her computer screen and made her way over to James' office. Considering the mess she found herself in the last time James offered her a job, Mollie felt understandably uneasy.

'What can I do for you?' She asked, allowing the heavy door to close behind her as she stepped into his office and took a seat opposite him.

'There's no need to look so worried.' Chuckling to himself as he collapsed into his plush chair, James smoothed down his tie. 'This one's a nice job. I promise.'

Not allowing herself to relax until she knew exactly what James was going to ask of her, Mollie bit her lip nervously.

'I was wondering if you could possibly spare a couple of hours this afternoon?' James said, smiling at Mollie from across his mahogany desk.

Being very aware that she didn't know what she was letting herself in for, Mollie chose her words carefully.

'I did plan on catching up with my correspondence this

afternoon.' She said slowly, trying her best to make this sound like the most important job on the planet. 'Is it urgent?'

'Pretty urgent.' Nodding as he spoke, James clasped his hands together in front of him. 'As I am sure you're aware, the office party is scheduled to start in a couple of hours, but due to the temping staff letting me down the boardroom is still minus the decorations Austin and I ordered...'

'I'll do it!' Mollie interrupted, unable to contain herself. 'I mean, I think I could *just* about squeeze it into my schedule.'

'Please don't feel obliged.' James added quickly. 'I can always ask one of the HR girls to do it.'

'No, no. I'll do it.' Smiling brightly, Mollie silently cheered at escaping her emails. 'Should I make a start on it right now?'

'If you could, that would be great.' James replied, scratching his stubble. 'I've arranged for the decorations, drinks and so forth to be delivered to the boardroom. Everything you need should already be in there.'

'Alright then.' Standing up, Mollie turned to leave and stopped when she realised that James was frowning intently. 'Was there anything else?'

Hesitating for a moment, James shook his head and turned back to his computer.

'No. That's everything.' He said decidedly. 'Thank you, Mollie.'

Taking this as her cue to leave, Mollie walked towards the door and stopped when he sighed heavily.

'Actually, there is something else.' James kept his gaze fixed on his computer screen and clicked his mouse repeatedly. 'But this is more of a *personal* matter.'

'Okay...' Mollie replied, slightly taken aback. 'What can I help you with?'

Obviously beating himself up for what he was about to say, James tapped his fingers on his desk and looked down at the ground thoughtfully. Being the kind of man who spoke solely about marketing proposals and Excel spreadsheets, the idea of him asking Mollie for advice on anything more personal than how he liked his coffee made her feel uncomfortable.

'Have you bought all of your Christmas gifts?' James asked, finally bringing his eyes up to meet Mollie's.

'Almost.' Mollie lied, not wanting to enter into a debate about her no-Christmas Christmas. 'Why do you ask?'

Loosening his tie, James' voice became oddly strangled as he squirmed uncomfortably in his seat.

'I... erm... a friend of mine is struggling to find a gift for his partner and he could really do with some help.' He stammered, his cheeks burning like hot lava. 'He's come to me for advice, but I don't know what to tell him. When it comes to gifts, I generally have Joyce send some flowers or a bottle of Rémy Martin, but I don't think that's going to hit the spot with this one.'

James' uncomfortable disposition was fascinating to Mollie as she watched the usually confident man dab his forehead with a handkerchief.

'Maybe it would help if I knew a bit about who the gift is for?' Mollie suggested, watching James twirl his gold pen around his fingers.

Nodding in agreement, James tapped his pen against the desk and took a deep breath.

'It's for a friend of mine.' He said, clearing his throat. 'A different friend from the one who is buying the gift, obviously.'

'Right.' Wondering why James was acting so out of character, Mollie studied his face carefully. 'And what are they like, this friend of yours?'

Despite his attempts to stop it, a slight smile played on James' lips as he leaned back in his seat and looked up at the ceiling.

'He's a workaholic, for a start.' He said, laughing lightly. 'He lives for his job. He's *always* working. He built his business up from scratch, so he takes it really seriously. Although, he isn't always so serious. There's a side to him that he doesn't let many people see.'

'And what's that side like?' Mollie asked quietly, not wanting to disrupt James' flow now that he was talking freely.

'It's the polar opposite of who people perceive him to be. He's secretly a whole world of fun. He likes to sing. *Loves* to sing. He sings at every chance he gets. You should hear him in the shower. And he rules the karaoke, but he would kill me if he knew I had told anyone that.' James paused to laugh and ran his fingers through his slicked-back hair. 'He's a great guy, and Christmas is the time to let him know just how amazing he is, right?'

'Right.' Surprised to hear her boss talking so passionately, Mollie offered him a smile across the desk.

'He's kind too.' James continued, completely unprompted. 'He does so much charity work. All anonymous. He doesn't want an ounce of recognition for it. He's overly generous and forever thoughtful. Always puts everyone else before himself. He's a *really* special man...'

As James' voice trailed off, Mollie noticed he was staring through the window. Following his gaze, she looked over her shoulder and felt her jaw drop open upon discovering he was looking directly at Austin Carter.

Quickly composing himself when he realised that Mollie had caught him staring, James coughed and sat up straight.

'So, do you have any ideas?' He asked, resting his elbows on the desk in front of him. 'As I said earlier, I'm asking for a friend.'

Completely lost for words, Mollie opened and closed her mouth repeatedly. There had been many occasions in her life when she had put two and two together and come up with a million, but this time, Mollie was pretty sure she was right on the money.

'I... err... erm...' Struggling to regain the use of her tongue, Mollie's eyes landed on James' briefcase. 'Briefcase! I would get him a briefcase.'

'A briefcase.' James repeated, attempting to return to his usual stern voice and failing. 'I suppose I could get... I mean... *they* could get him a briefcase.'

Not knowing where to look, Mollie felt the elephant in the room grow bigger and bigger until it was impossible to ignore.

'Should I make a start on the boardroom?' She asked, twisting her wedding ring around her finger and keeping her gaze fixed firmly on the floor.

'That would be great.' Turning back to his computer, James gave Mollie a nod and pretended to be engrossed in his emails. 'Thank you, Mollie.'

Offering him an equally serious nod in response, Mollie

started to walk away and stopped when she reached the door.

'James?' She said, pausing with her hand on the door handle. 'If this friend is as special as you say he is, forget the briefcase and just let him know. As you said before, Christmas is the time to let people know just how much they mean to us.'

Holding eye contact for a moment too long, James' eyes flickered to Austin once more before returning to his computer.

'Joyce had the key to the boardroom earlier.' He replied, any emotion he displayed before now absent from his voice. 'It should still be open.'

With a final smile, Mollie let herself out and made her way across the office floor. Utterly blown away by the conversation she had just shared with James, she felt her skin tingle with adrenaline. The mysterious but affable manager that was James Payne was somewhat of an enigma. For as long as Mollie had worked for Payne and Carter, she hadn't ever dived into the man behind the suit. She knew what he liked for breakfast, she knew that he always left work at three o'clock on Fridays, and she knew that he secretly played Candy Crush on his phone during meetings. What she didn't know was anything about his life outside of working hours.

James Payne was very much a closed book. If it didn't concern Payne and Carter, James simply didn't talk about it. The idea of Payne and Carter being partners inside and outside the office made Mollie feel all warm and fuzzy inside. Being a pair of good-looking, successful, career-driven men, there was no doubting that they would make a gorgeous couple, but their compatibility was suddenly glaringly obvious to Mollie. She simply hadn't seen it before because she had put them firmly into the *boss* category and not given a second thought to who they were when they walked out of the door.

Mollie wholeheartedly believed that Christmas was a special time that united friends and family. Knowing what she now knew, she could only hope that the magic of Christmas would bring Payne and Carter together too...

Chapter Fourteen

Completely thrown by James' not-so-discreet declaration of love for his business partner, Mollie exhaled loudly as she came to a stop outside the boardroom. Discovering it was unlocked, she let herself in and studied the empty space before her. The boardroom looked exactly as it usually did, except for a collection of cardboard boxes that were piled high on the huge oval table.

Lifting the lid on one of the many boxes, Mollie smiled when she discovered more foil decorations than even Mrs Heckles' could handle. If the dated tinsel was anything to go by, James and Austin had been rolling out the same decorations since the company opened its doors over twenty years ago.

Plucking a gold garland out of the nearest box, she draped it around her neck and moved on to the next. Dozens of glass bottles and red paper cups were waiting patiently to be unleashed. If she listened carefully, she could almost hear them tapping their feet as they counted down the minutes until party time.

After sticking her nose into all of the boxes, Mollie hopped onto the table and pulled her phone out of her back pocket. Bringing up Tim's work number, she held the handset against her ear and waited to hear his familiar voice.

'Tim Slease.'

'It's me.' Mollie said, swinging her legs back and forth. 'Do you think you can sneak away for a little while?'

'If you want me to carry any more Christmas trees, forget it.'

'It's nothing to do with Christmas trees.' Reaching into one of the decoration-filled boxes at her feet, Mollie chose a bottle of brandy and studied the label. 'Well, it *is* to do with Christmas.'

'I don't know, Molls.' Tim said hesitantly. 'Whenever you

ask for my help, I always seem to find myself in a situation that HR would most definitely disapprove of.'

'Just come to the boardroom.' Mollie instructed, placing the brandy back into the box and pulling out a bottle of rum. 'And try not to get seen on the way.'

Knowing this would get Tim sweating, Mollie giggled and ended the call. With just two hours to transform the boardroom into a party-worthy space, she needed as much help as she could get. The stack of boxes on the floor trembled as Mollie jumped off the table and began sorting the pieces of tinsel into colour-coded piles. Before long, the boardroom table was completely covered beneath a sea of old-fashioned decorations.

As Mollie grabbed a few random pieces of green tinsel to dress the windows, she heard the door open behind her.

'Slease!' She giggled, covering her mouth with her hand as Tim stepped into the room. 'What are you wearing?'

'You clearly stated that I was not to get seen!' Tim's muffled voice drifted out from behind the stick-on beard, causing Mollie to laugh even harder. 'This was the best I could do at a moment's notice.'

Wearing Joyce's Secret Santa hat, a white beard and his trademark black mac, Tim couldn't have looked more obvious if he tried.

'Only because I didn't want you to get into trouble for skiving!' Mollie said, taking the Santa hat and placing it on her own head. 'But now that you're here, this get-up is quite fitting.'

'Just so you know, Molls, I meant what I said about the Christmas tree.' Tim said firmly. 'I was a nervous wreck the other day worrying that Arnold would find it in the storeroom. Thankfully, I managed to convince him that the lock was broken, but I did have to unplug his phone to stop him from calling the caretaker to complain. The whole thing was very stressful for me.'

'There shall be no trees, Tim. You have my word.' Using a handful of drawing pins to secure a piece of tinsel against the window frame, Mollie pointed to the boxes on the floor. 'James has asked me to decorate the boardroom for the party later. I thought you might want to escape Arnold for a while and give me a hand.'

'Oh, then count me in.' Visibly breathing a sigh of relief, Tim pulled off the beard and dropped it onto one of the many chairs. 'Apart from the tree we decorated when we emptied Mum's house, I haven't really bothered to put up any decorations this year.'

'Any reason why?' Mollie asked, draping an assortment of silver tinsel over the photocopier.

'I'm still finding my feet, I guess.' Rooting through the box of spirits, Tim read the label on a bottle of vodka and shrugged. 'It feels a little strange to be living on my own again.'

'I'm sure it does.' Mollie offered Tim a smile and studied her friend's face closely. 'How are you finding being in your own company?'

'Believe it or not, Molls, I'm really enjoying it.' Tim replied, placing the vodka back into the box. 'I had become so used to doing everything for Mum that I had forgotten how to look after myself. Now, I get home from work and wonder what I am going to do with my spare time.'

Listening to Tim speak, Mollie wrapped a piece of tinsel around her wrist.

'I suppose I am getting to know myself again.' He continued. 'I've started running. I'm learning a new language. I'm even going to exhibitions. There just wasn't enough hours in the day before. By the time I had made sure Mum was okay, all there was time to do was collapse into bed and hope I didn't sleep through my alarm.'

Tim paused for breath and looked over at Mollie guiltily.

'Does that make me the most selfish person on the planet?' He asked sheepishly.

'Not in the slightest!' Mollie exclaimed, resting her hands on her hips. 'You are the most selfless person I've ever met, Tim. You deserve to find happiness more than anyone.'

'That's the thing.' Tim replied. 'I miss Mum like crazy, but I really am happy.'

'Well, I'm happy that you're happy, and I know that Dottie would be too.' Smiling at Tim from across the room, Mollie felt a swell of pride at how well her friend had coped with his mother's passing. 'Good for you, Slease.'

An emotional silence fell over the boardroom until Mollie broke it by turning the radio on.

'So, what language are you learning?' She asked, reaching for yet more decorations. 'French? Spanish? German?'

'Japanese.' Stepping onto a chair to hang a foil garland from the light fitting, Tim bowed his head to Mollie. 'Konnichiwa.'

'*Konnichiwa* right back at you.' She replied, not having a clue what she had just said. 'What about these exhibitions you've been going to? Anything interesting?'

'It's actually just one exhibition, but I have been to it numerous times.' Tim explained. 'Four, to be precise.'

'Four times?' Mollie asked. 'What is it?'

'The National Pokémon Convention.' Jumping down from the chair, Tim grabbed a handful of tinsel and began tying random pieces to the backs of chairs. 'I've always wanted to go, but I've never been able to justify the expense. I'm finally allowing myself a little indulgence.'

Nodding in response, Mollie sighed happily as she watched Tim create perfect bows out of the retro decorations. Despite the cruel twists and turns that Tim's life had taken, some things would never change. Timothy Slease had always had a funny way of looking at the world, but it meant that he saw things from a different perspective to everyone else. It meant that he appreciated what most people took for granted and noticed things others didn't.

Tossing the piece of tinsel that she was holding back into the box, Mollie leaned against the photocopier as a thought suddenly hit her.

'Tim?' She said, sidling over to where he was sitting. 'How long have you worked for Payne and Carter?'

'Too long.' Tim answered, taking the gold piece of tinsel from around Mollie's neck and wrapping it around a chair. 'Why do you ask?'

'I'm just making conversation.' Smiling innocently, Mollie began to unpack the many bottles of spirits onto the table. 'Out of interest, was it James or Austin who conducted your interview?'

'It was actually Austin and Eddie.' Tim answered casually. 'I believe I was the last person Eddie hired before he handed the reins over to James.'

'You remember James joining the company?' Trying to disguise her eagerness to discover what he knew about James and Austin, Mollie forced a yawn. 'What was he like back then?'

'I do.' Tim replied. 'And he was exactly the same as he is now, just with less grey hairs.'

'I can't imagine him without his silver streaks.' Mollie peeled the cellophane off a pack of paper cups and placed them next to the rows of spirits. 'Do you happen to know if he has any children?'

'Not that I know of.' Shaking his head, Tim chose a handful of purple tinsel. 'He did have a guy that used to come and visit him quite frequently, but he was too old to be a son.'

Pursing her lips, Mollie gave Tim a single nod in response and opened another pack of cups.

'Was he married back then?' She asked, before she could stop herself. 'I've noticed that he doesn't wear a ring, but that doesn't mean he hasn't been married in the past. Actually, he *could* be married and just chooses not to wear a ring.'

Looking up from the makeshift bar, Mollie frowned when she realised that Tim was staring at her with a rather amused look on his face.

'I think someone might have a little crush on James.' Tim said teasingly. 'But I have to say, Molls, he's a little bit old for you.'

'I don't have a crush on James!' Mollie retorted, not wanting to confess to having developed crushes on both James *and* Austin in the past. 'I'm just curious about the firm's history, that's all.'

'I think one protests too much.' Tim persisted. 'Look at you! Your cheeks are redder than those cups!'

'You're being ridiculous.' Feeling her face burn, Mollie made a stab at changing the subject. 'Anyway, how is Heidi doing? Still frolicking around San Antonio?'

'Nope. She's now in Cala Llonga.' Taking a pack of paper tablecloths from one of the boxes, Tim began to pile the remaining decorations on the floor. 'She sent some pictures of a property that she had set her heart on, but the lease fell through at the last minute.'

'That's a shame.' Mollie replied, joining Tim in clearing the table. 'Any reason why?'

Collapsing one of the cardboard boxes, Tim placed it next to the door and rubbed his lower back.

'The building was occupied by a knitting group on Saturdays.' He explained. 'It seems the manager was a little concerned about the two groups, you know, crossing paths.'

'I suppose that's understandable.' Mollie said, trying not to laugh. 'Tantric sex and knitting clubs are miles apart on the hobby spectrum.'

'You would be surprised, Molls.' Shaking out a tablecloth, Tim draped it over the table and made an attempt at smoothing out the creases. 'A lot of Heidi's clients are at the upper end of seventy.'

Visibly gulping, Mollie grabbed a bottle of brandy and quickly whipped off the lid.

'Let's have a sneaky drink to get us in the party mood.' She said, desperate to erase the knitting class conversation from her memory. 'This brandy has been calling out to me since I walked in here.'

'The party doesn't start for another...' Studying his watch, Tim frowned and pulled a string of fairy lights out of one of the remaining boxes. 'Seventy-three minutes.'

'Don't be such a party pooper!' Mollie demanded, pouring herself a tiny short. 'James won't mind.'

'I think James will always mind his staff drinking during working hours.' Giving Mollie a knowing look, Tim wagged a finger sternly. 'Christmas or no Christmas.'

Not being deterred, Mollie raised the glass to her lips as Tim looked on disapprovingly.

'You're making me an accomplice.' He warned. 'You do know that, don't you?'

'Wait until I ask you to hide the evidence.' Mollie whispered playfully. 'Then you'll be an accessory after the fact.'

'To be honest, Molls, I think my position in this scenario leans more towards hostage.' Carrying the fairy lights across the room, Tim headed for the nearest free plug socket. 'You're officially a hostage-taker.'

'Hey, you came here of your own free will.' Taking a generous sip from her paper cup, Mollie jumped down from the table and gathered the cellophane wrappers. 'You're free to leave at any time.'

'Even so, I'm having nothing to do with it.' Tim shook his head and plugged in the lights next to the photocopier.

'Come on, Slease! Don't think of it as drinking during working hours.' She said encouragingly. 'Think of it as quality control. We're preparing for the party, and part of that preparation is ensuring that the drinks are up to scratch.'

Pausing with the fairy lights in his hands, Tim lowered his eyes to the cup in Mollie's hand.

'This could all be contaminated.' Mollie continued, demonstrating towards the impressive selection of booze. 'You would be doing James a huge favour. Just think of the lawsuit you would be saving him from if there *is* anything terrible lurking in these bottles.'

'Fine.' Tim conceded. 'I will have a drink with you if you tell me why you're so interested in James Payne.'

'I'm just curious about the company's history.' Mollie lied. 'I've already told you that.'

'I believe that as much as I believe Kenny is five-foot-ten.' Tim fired back. 'So, are you going to spill the beans?'

Recalling her conversation with James, Mollie poured another brandy and pushed the cup towards Tim.

'If I tell you, you have to promise to keep this between us.' Mollie instructed, pointing her finger seriously. 'Okay?'

'Scout's honour.' Tim replied, staring at Mollie with bated breath as he waited for the bombshell to drop.

Touching her paper cup against Tim's, Mollie permitted herself one more sip before speaking.

'I believe that James Payne may have a *thing* going on with someone in the office.' She squealed. 'Can you believe it?'

'A thing?' Tim repeated. 'What kind of thing?'

'You know!' Mollie hissed. 'A *thing* thing!'

'Right.' Tim said, seemingly losing all interest. 'And?'

'Don't you want to know who with?' Mollie exclaimed. 'It's pretty huge.'

'Nope.' Returning to the photocopier, Tim picked up the flashing fairy lights. 'Where do you want these?'

Not being deterred by Tim's nonchalant reaction, Mollie followed him around the table.

'Slease, this will floor you!' She persisted. 'I *never* saw this coming! Of all the people in this company, I never would have guessed that...'

'Molls?' Tim interrupted. 'I hate to disappoint you, but I have no interest in knowing idle office gossip about our boss.'

Slightly taken aback by Tim's no-nonsense response to her shock piece of information, Mollie opened her mouth to protest further.

'But...'

'Heidi always says that you shouldn't spread with your mouth what you haven't seen with your eyes.' He warned, draping the fairy lights over the photocopier. 'Anyway, I wouldn't have thought that gossiping really fit in with your no-Christmas Christmas pledge?'

Resisting the urge to inform Tim that she *had* seen it with her own eyes, Mollie looked into her cup guiltily.

'You're right.' She said. 'Christmas is a time to spread goodwill and joy, not silly rumours.'

Nodding in agreement, Tim abandoned his fairy lights and walked over to where Mollie was standing.

'Very true, but I suppose Christmas is also a time when it's acceptable to drink at otherwise unacceptable times.' He added, holding his paper cup in the air. 'Merry Christmas, Molls.'

Grinning back at him, Mollie clinked her cup against his and turned up the volume on the radio.

'Merry Christmas, Slease.'

Chapter Fifteen

The Christmas classics everyone knew and loved pumped out of the speakers as the boardroom became the stage for the party the employees of Payne and Carter had waited all year for. With enough drinks to fill an Olympic swimming pool being poured out by eager members of staff who were determined to fill their boots, the boardroom was unrecognisable.

Mollie found it hard to believe that it was the same space she and Tim had dressed for the occasion just a few hours earlier. Groups of people were dancing around the table, the buffet was being raided, and the HR girls were posing for selfies next to the Christmas tree. It was only a matter of time before someone started the infamous Payne and Carter conga line.

Sitting next to Tim at the far end of the room, Mollie tapped her foot in time to the music and admired their handiwork. The tinsel Tim had painstakingly tied to the back of each chair was now being used as a series of interesting accessories. Neil from accounts had draped a piece around his neck in place of his tie, Elise from HR had made herself a questionable halo, and a woman whom Mollie didn't recognise was using a piece to lasso various different men onto the makeshift dance floor.

Squinting in a bid to see clearly in the dimly lit room, Mollie realised that the dancing queen was actually Susan from finance. Without their usual shirts and blazers, Mollie was having a hard time recognising her colleagues. It was like witnessing Superman without his cape. They all just looked a little... *weird*. Arnold was wearing Dr Martens, Joyce was trundling around in shoes with an actual kitten heel, and Neil appeared to be wearing a rather hefty dose of eyeliner.

Before Mollie could raise the subject of Neil's incredible cosmetology skills, Tim handed her a paper plate.

'You have to try this Yule log!' He yelled, struggling to be heard over the sound of Mariah Carey. 'Joyce made it herself.'

Pulling the plate towards her, Mollie licked a dollop of

brandy cream off her finger and took a huge bite. With her mouth filled with chocolatey goodness, Mollie flashed Tim the thumbs-up sign and sank into her seat. Her obsession with throwing a no-Christmas Christmas meant that she hadn't allowed herself to indulge in any of her usual festive faves. Therefore, Mollie wanted to savour every moment.

'When do you think they will start the Secret Santa?' Tim asked, wiping his mouth on a napkin.

Glancing across the room at the impressive arrangement of presents, Mollie shrugged her shoulders. The staffroom dining table had been covered with a red tablecloth, and was adorned with dozens of mystery gifts. Scouring the mountain of presents for the gold envelope she dropped into the Santa sack earlier, Mollie noticed Joyce signalling for the music to be turned down.

'May I have your attention, please?' Joyce said gloomily, positioning herself at the head of the room. 'The Secret Santa is now open. Come and find your name at your leisure. First come, first served.'

'You must be psychic.' Mollie said to Tim, who was already climbing out of his seat like a child on Christmas Day.

'You're not the first person to say that to me, Molls.' Brushing the remnants of his Yule log off his Christmas jumper, Tim frowned when he realised his fingers were now covered in chocolate. 'I saw a nail standing upright in the street last week and I just *knew* there would be a problem with sharp objects somewhere down the road. It was a sign. I could feel it in my bones.'

'And what happened?' Mollie asked, genuinely intrigued.

'The knitting class!' Tim exclaimed. 'Heidi's tantric sex retreat fell through because of the knitting class!'

'Right...' Mollie replied uncertainly. 'I see.'

'I should really start writing these things down.' He mused, licking chocolate off his fingers. 'I've been blessed with a remarkable gift. I could be the next Derek Acorah.'

Watching Tim scurry over to the table of gifts, Mollie laughed before pushing out her chair and joining him at the Secret Santa station. Dozens of beautifully wrapped gifts were piled high as various members of staff took great pleasure in scouring the many anonymous boxes in search of their name.

'Found mine!' Tim cheered, waving a small box in the air. 'Any luck finding yours, Molls?'

Rifling through the glittering boxes, Mollie turned over name tag after name tag until she spotted her name scrawled on a purple gift bag.

'Got it!' She said, following Tim through the crowd and returning to her seat. 'You open yours first.'

Collapsing into the chair next to Mollie, Tim attempted to carefully remove the Sellotape before giving in and ripping off the wrapping paper like a wild animal who had finally found food.

'What is it?' Mollie asked, leaning over Tim's shoulder to get a better view of what had caused his jaw to fall open.

'It's... it's...' Seemingly lost for words, Tim turned a transparent box around for Mollie to see for herself.

'A Pokémon card?' Mollie squinted at the box that Tim was holding out and frowned. 'Is that what it is?'

'It isn't *just* a Pokémon card, Molls!' Tim stammered in a bid to get his words out as he clutched the card as though it was a winning lottery ticket. 'It's one of the rarest Pokémon cards there is. I don't understand. This must have cost...'

'Seven pounds and thirty-three pence.' Arnold announced, coming to a stop in front of Tim and grinning proudly. 'Well within the designated limit. I found it on eBay. The seller obviously didn't know what he had. He even threw in the presentation box.'

Looking up at Arnold in awe, Tim held the presentation box against his chest and laughed in disbelief.

'I don't believe it.' He gushed. 'I've been looking for this for years! This is the best present I've ever had. Thank you, Arnold. Thank you so much.'

Stuffing his hands into the pockets of his ripped jeans, Arnold shrugged his shoulders bashfully.

'Merry Christmas, Tim.' He said. 'You too, Mollie.'

'Merry Christmas, Arnold.' Tim and Mollie replied in unison.

Tipping his bottle of beer towards them, Arnold turned around and joined an enthusiastic Susan on the dance floor.

'So, I take it you're happy with your Secret Santa gift?' Mollie said, twisting in her chair to face Tim.

'Happy? I'm ecstatic!' He cried. 'This is the best Christmas ever! Let's see what's in yours!'

Doing as she was instructed, Mollie tucked her hair behind her ears and dived into the gift bag. Her hand landed on a mound of pink tissue paper that was protecting the rather heavy object beneath. Placing the shredded paper on the table, Mollie peered into the bag before pulling out a slim glass bottle. Turning it over in her hands, she used the torch on her phone to read the writing on the label.

'Christmas Spirit.' She read aloud. 'With notes of figs, clementines, Christmas pudding and cinnamon, this limited edition room spray is Christmas in a bottle. The perfect way to rediscover the magic of Christmas.'

'How very apt.' Tim remarked, taking the bottle from Mollie and spraying it into the air.

'A little too apt.' Narrowing her eyes at him, Mollie sniffed the nozzle on the bottle and nodded appreciatively. 'Did you have something to do with this?'

'Molls, I can solemnly swear that I am categorically *not* your Secret Santa.' Tim said convincingly. 'But I may have given Elise a slight nudge in the right direction.'

Smelling the nozzle once more, Mollie caught Elise's eye from across the room and mouthed *thank you.*

'Compared to the complimentary AA road map I received in last year's Secret Santa, this is like hitting the jackpot.' She said, reaching for her drink. 'Plus, if Max burns the turkey like he did last year, this will come in handy. Let's just hope it isn't a premonition.'

Laughing along, Tim placed his Pokémon card into the safety of his laptop bag.

'I hope our Secret Santa gifts have been as well received.' He mused, reaching for his drink.

Automatically looking over at Joyce, Mollie watched as the receptionist hovered next to the Secret Santa station until everyone else had taken their gifts. The once overflowing pile of presents had been reduced to a single gold envelope in the centre of the table. Slowly walking towards it, Joyce peeked at the name before picking it up and slowly retreating into a dark corner of the room. The sound of Neil and Susan singing along to the music filled the vast room as Joyce opened the envelope and held it close to her face.

'Correct me if I am wrong, but I believe Joyce is smiling.' Tim said uncertainly, leaning forwards in his chair for a closer look. 'On second thoughts, she may just have wind because I've seen Uncle Ben pull a face like that before he...'

'I'm pretty sure that's a smile, Slease.' Mollie interrupted. 'At least, I hope it is.'

'Do you think she has a rare Pokémon card too?' He gasped, his eyes widening. 'I've got to find out...'

'It's not a Pokémon card, Tim!' Grabbing his arm before he could race over to Joyce, Mollie pulled Tim back into his seat. 'It's an invite. I invited her to join us for Christmas. *I'm* her Secret Santa.'

'You invited Joyce?' Tim asked in disbelief. 'For Christmas? You invited grumpy old Joyce to your house at Christmas?'

'I sure did.' Mollie replied. 'Within the designated budget, and as long as Max follows the dairy-free recipes I gave him, it won't interfere with Joyce's lactose intolerance.'

'Wow, Molls.' Completely taken aback by Mollie's kind gesture, Tim looked on as Joyce excitedly took her envelope around the boardroom and showed anyone who would look. 'That's *really* nice of you.'

Shrugging her shoulders, Mollie took a sip from her paper cup and smiled as a warmth of happiness rushed through her veins. Joyce's gift hadn't cost Mollie a penny, she hadn't had to brave the shops for it, and she hadn't felt the need to put a receipt in the back just in case Joyce wanted to return it. Mollie had given Joyce the one gift that money couldn't buy, which made it all the more sweeter.

'Well, if Austin is smiling half as much as Joyce is, I think we can safely say that Secret Santa has been a success all around.' Tim said happily. 'Any idea where he is?'

Scouring the boardroom, Mollie nudged Tim when she spotted Austin and James in the far corner of the room. Despite their attempts to look inconspicuous, the slick suits they were wearing made them stand out like a pair of sore thumbs amongst the rabble of sparkly dresses and Christmas jumpers. Due to the incredibly loud music that was now pumping out of the speakers, Mollie couldn't hear a single word they were saying, but her position at the head of the table gave her a perfect view of the scene that was unfolding between the two CEOs.

The smiles on their faces were bright enough to light up the room, but even in the dark Mollie could see there was a hint of hesitation in James' eyes. As she looked on, James reached to the floor and produced a large box, which he cautiously handed to Austin. Mollie held her breath as Austin placed his paper cup on the windowsill before removing the lid and peeling back the dust bag. While Austin unwrapped his gift, Mollie shifted her focus to James. His dark eyes stared at Austin intently, as though they were the only two people in the crowded room.

Smiling brightly, Austin reached into the box and retrieved a sleek briefcase before embracing James in a warm hug. The two men held each other for a moment before quickly dusting themselves down and returning to their drinks. As they tapped their paper cups together, James paused before reaching into his pocket and holding out a tiny card. Flashing James a confused look, Austin exchanged his cup for the card and turned towards the window. Moonlight shone onto the card through the open blinds as he tilted it from left to right in a bid to read what had been written inside.

Not daring to breathe, Mollie cursed as Susan dragged Neil onto the dance floor and blocked her view entirely. Straining her neck in a bid to see how Austin would react to James' mystery card, Mollie was treated to the sight of Susan and Neil doing the Macarena. Just as she was preparing to dive out of her seat and clear the obstacles with a fury she had only ever unleashed on a coughing cinemagoer at the anniversary screening of Dirty Dancing, Susan and Neil disappeared into a corner of their own.

Blinking in a bid to see clearly in the shadowy room, Mollie sighed with disappointment when she discovered that the card was now nowhere to be seen, but the expressions on James and Austin's faces told her everything she needed to know. It was no longer just their suits that were matching. Their smiles were identical, their eyes had the same fuzzy glint, and they were mirroring one another's body language perfectly.

Lowering her gaze, Mollie gasped out loud when she realised they were holding hands.

'Tim!' She hissed, her voice high with excitement for James and Austin. 'Can you see this?'

Not getting a response, she nudged Tim so hard that he almost fell off his chair.

'*Tim!*'

Looking mightily confused, Tim rubbed his arm and frowned.

'There's been some kind of mix-up.' He said in bewilderment. 'I didn't get Austin a briefcase. I need to go and find Joyce.'

Rolling her eyes, Mollie laughed and held out her hand for Tim's empty cup.

'Well, before you report this serious offence to the Secret Santa police, let's go and get another drink...'

Chapter Sixteen

Looking up at the rather clinical building before her, Mollie rubbed her hands together for warmth and studied the faded sign above the door. The snow was falling thick and fast, creating a blizzard of snowflakes in front of Mollie's face as she tried to calculate if they had followed Eugenie's directions correctly. When Mollie agreed to meet Eugenie at the Rainbow Volunteer Group that Saturday, she envisaged a rather quaint building surrounded by trees and fairy-filled woodland. The newly built office block they had arrived at could have been home to anything from an accountant's office to an awfully sterile library.

Not wanting to get off on the wrong foot, Mollie forced herself to remain positive.

'Are you sure this is the place?' Max asked, obviously having the same doubts. 'It's not quite what I was expecting.'

'According to the map, we have arrived at our destination.' Waiting for Tim to catch up with them, Mollie watched a young woman walk into the building and checked the address once more. 'This is definitely it.'

Hearing footsteps behind her, Mollie looked over her shoulder to see Tim racing across the road.

'Sorry about that.' He said, panting for breath. 'The battery in this pedometer is supposed to last for five years. I've only had it for four. I must remember to check the warranty when I get home.'

'Does Heidi check your step count every day?' Max asked, following Mollie as she led the way towards the building.

'She does indeed.' Tim confirmed. 'It's linked to hers, and if she doesn't see ten thousand steps she is not a happy bunny, hence why I had to dash off in search of a replacement battery.'

'Did you manage to find one?' Max asked, failing to disguise his amusement.

'I did. Luckily, the newspaper stand back there had one pack of AAA batteries left. I thought it took AA, but hey, you learn something new every day.' Wiping his brow on his sleeve, Tim checked his pedometer for confirmation it was working. 'We're good to go.'

'Alright then.' Clapping her hands together, Mollie paused in front of the clinical green door. 'Is everyone ready?'

Max and Tim cheered simultaneously as Mollie cast aside her doubts and pushed her way inside. The yellow walls radiated a warmth around the welcoming reception room as they headed towards the smiling receptionist.

'Hi.' Mollie said, coming to a stop in front of the plastic desk. 'We're here to volunteer.'

'Fantastic!' Spinning around in her chair, the pretty receptionist grabbed a clipboard from the filing cabinet behind her. 'If you could fill these out for me, I shall get you all registered.'

'There's no need for that, Sascha.' A familiar voice quipped. 'I've already done them.'

Spinning around, Mollie grinned when she spotted Eugenie striding into the reception area with three clipboards under her arm. Wearing a pair of baggy jeans, her usual Converse and a knitted poncho, Eugenie made a beeline for the receptionist.

'Mollie, Max and Tim.' Eugenie announced, placing the completed paperwork on the reception desk. 'Is it okay if I take them through?'

After giving the clipboards a cursory glance, Sascha nodded and gave Eugenie the thumbs-up sign.

'Come on, guys!' Eugenie said happily, beckoning for them to follow her. 'Let me show you around.'

Smiling politely at Sascha, Mollie and the guys traced Eugenie's footsteps through a set of double doors. The second they stepped over the threshold, the entire outside world melted away. Mollie and the guys soon discovered that the sterile exterior of the building was not an indication of what was inside. The far wall was covered in a series of beautiful thank you cards, creating a collage of heartfelt keepsakes. A television was playing in the left-hand corner of the room while a gaggle of elderly ladies leisurely chatted with their eyes glued to the screen. A couple of grey-haired gentlemen were playing a game of chess next to the window, and a few workmen in high-visibility jackets were talking animatedly in the old kitchenette.

'So, welcome to Rainbows.' Eugenie said, her glossy hair shining under the bright lights. 'You guys are a little late, so we're going to get straight to it.'

'That's my fault.' Tim confessed sheepishly. 'I had a problem with my pedometer.'

Eugenie frowned in confusion, and Mollie gave her a look which said *don't ask*.

'Anyway...' Eugenie replied slowly. 'Max, you are up first.'

Suddenly looking rather nervous, Max folded his arms as he waited to hear what task he had been allocated to.

'Rupert?' Eugenie shouted in the direction of the kitchenette. 'We're ready for you.'

Raising his hand, a middle-aged man wearing a neon tabard walked across the room to join them.

'Rupert, this is Max.' Eugenie explained, tactfully moving out of the way as Max and Rupert shook hands. 'He's going with you.'

'Going?' Max repeated, looking at Rupert for a clue as to what was happening. 'Going where?'

'We're going to put those muscles to use, young man.' Patting Max on the back, Rupert passed him a pair of heavy-duty gloves. 'Ready to shovel some snow?'

'You are going to help Rupert clear the driveways of some vulnerable residents in the area.' Eugenie explained, obviously enjoying her role as chief organiser. 'How do you feel about that?'

Clearly relieved that his task didn't involve a shopping centre, a gang of children on sugar highs or an elf costume, Max smiled with relief.

'That sounds good to me.' He said, tugging on the gloves. 'Any chance of a coffee first?'

'We have flasks ready and waiting in the car.' Rupert replied. 'If you're really lucky, you might get a biscuit from Mrs Phillips on Walton Street.'

'Biscuits and coffee? I think I'll volunteer more often.' Rubbing his hands together, Max followed Rupert to the exit. 'See you later, guys!'

'Will my job involve biscuits and coffee too?' Tim asked, mournfully watching them leave. 'I could do with something to warm me up. I missed breakfast this morning. It's years since I last left the house without my pickled egg. I actually feel a little woozy. My blood sugar levels are probably dropping as we speak.'

'It *shall* involve biscuits and coffee.' Knowing how dramatic Tim could be, Eugenie passed him a boiled sweet and glossed over his comments. 'However, you shall be *shopping* for them, *not* eating them.'

Beckoning him to follow her, Eugenie led them over to where the knitting ladies were sitting.

'Tim, I would like you to meet Olive.'

Immediately looking up from the television, a plump lady with a fabulous blue rinse smiled brightly.

'Hello, Olive.' Tim said politely. 'It's a pleasure to meet you.'

'Are you the young man who will be helping me with my shopping today?' Olive asked, pulling her handbag onto her lap.

'That's correct.' Eugenie replied on his behalf. 'Tim, how do you feel about accompanying Olive to the supermarket this morning?'

'I would love to.' Holding out a hand to help Olive to her feet, Tim gave her a quick courtesy. 'Are you an Aldi girl or would you prefer a bit of the old Marks and Spencer?'

A chorus of impressed *oohs* echoed around Olive's group of pals at the mention of Marks and Spencer.

'Oh, I do love Marks and Spencer.' Olive gushed enthusiastically. 'We all do, but it is way across town. We have to take two buses just to get there. Volunteers usually only have an hour, so it's rare we get a visit to M&S.'

'Luckily for you, I have all day.' Tim replied. 'Marks and Spencer it is. That should put a few miles on the old pedometer.'

Before Olive could express her gratitude, she was inundated with requests from her friends for elusive Marks and Spencer produce.

'Could you get me a pair of those opaque tights that I like in a medium?' The lady on her left asked, frantically opening her purse and passing Olive a perfectly folded note. 'Actually, you better get a large. Cora is making her bread and butter pudding for Christmas lunch, so I could do with the extra room.'

'Large.' Olive repeated, slipping the note into her bra. 'Got it.'

'If you happen to see any of those thermal vests that Beryl wears, grab me a couple in black.' Another woman chipped in, shaking some coins out of her purse and pushing them towards Olive. 'You know my size, right?'

Cupping her hands around her mouth, Olive whispered something to her friend.

'Perfect.' The friend said. 'Keep the change for your troubles.'

'Should we club together and get some of those cherry liqueurs for Hannah at the retirement home?' Olive suggested. 'It would be a nice little Christmas pressie for her, you know, to say thank you for everything she does for us all year.'

The rest of the ladies eagerly agreed as Olive began to calculate how much each person owed.

'I think you're going to need a list.' Eugenie whispered to Tim, offering him a notepad. 'Let me get Mollie set up and I shall come back and see how you're getting on.'

Leaving Tim writing down orders, Eugenie linked her arm through Mollie's and led her to the other side of the room.

'I've saved the best until last for you, Mollie.' Eugenie said. 'After all, we're only here because of you.'

'That sounds intriguing.' Mollie replied, looking around the room for a hint as to where Eugenie was taking her. 'As long as it doesn't involve a grotto, you can count me in.'

'In that case, I would like you to meet Herbert.' Coming to a stop at a small table next to the window, Eugenie placed her left hand on an elderly gentleman's shoulder. 'Herbert here is looking for a helping hand with his Christmas cards.'

'Arthritis.' Herbert explained, holding up a withered hand. 'Just a quick squiggle will do. There aren't all that many.'

'I think we can do better than a quick squiggle.' Sitting down in the chair opposite him, Mollie winked at Eugenie as she slipped away to rescue Tim from Olive's gal pals. 'I did a calligraphy course back in my teenage years. I might be a bit rusty, but let's see what we can do.'

Rolling up her sleeves, Mollie pulled the stack of blank Christmas cards towards her.

'I'm Mollie, but the way.' She said, shuffling her seat closer to the table and reaching for a pen.

'Herbert.' Tipping his flat cap towards her, Herbert smiled politely. 'Herbert Baxter.'

'Well, it's a pleasure to meet you, Herbert Baxter. Let's get these Christmas cards done, shall we?'

'If you wouldn't mind, that would be fabulous.' He replied, pulling a crumpled sheet of paper from the pocket of his tweed jacket and smoothing it out on the table. 'The first name on the list is Vera Holland.'

'Vera Holland.' Mollie repeated. 'Any particular design?'

Spreading the array of Christmas cards out in front of him, Mollie waited for Herbert to make his selection.

'This one is nice.' She suggested, pointing to a picture of three snoozing kittens in front of a roaring fire.

'That'll do nicely.' Herbert agreed.

Mollie nodded in response and hovered the pen over the open card.

'Now that I think about it, Vera's allergic to cats.' Herbert said suddenly. 'Perhaps we should go with that one there.'

'This one?' Holding up the card that Herbert was pointing at, Mollie smiled at the rather comical image of a rotund Santa Claus wedged inside a chimney.

'Let's go with that one.' Herbert took off his cap and scratched his head uncertainly. 'Better to be on the safe side.'

'No problem.' Mollie replied happily. 'Choosing a card can be difficult. My grandma used to spend hours in Clintons browsing the aisles. She used to say that choosing a card was like paying a compliment. One wrong word and you can find yourself firmly in insult territory.'

Lowering his gaze to the card once more, Herbert shook his head.

'On second thoughts.' He said, tapping his walking stick on the floor. 'Vera's late husband had a gastric band fitted after getting stuck in a shower cubicle. That might be a little close to the bone.'

Swallowing the giggle that was desperately trying to escape her lips, Mollie smiled when she realised that Herbert had a mischievous glint in his eye.

'Okay. How about this one?' She offered, picking up a rather mundane card with the words *Merry Christmas* splashed across the front in gold lettering. 'There's absolutely nothing that can be misconstrued about this one.'

Studying the card for a moment, Herbert rubbed his temples.

'Why is this so bloody hard?' He complained. 'My Agatha used to deal with all of this. She would have had these sorted at the start of December. She thought of everything, right up until the end.'

Smiling sadly, Mollie placed her pen on the table and gave Herbert her full attention.

'She left me a whole bunch of lists.' He continued, pushing another crumbled piece of paper towards Mollie. 'There must have been a list for everything. How to use the washing machine, where the insurance documents are kept, how much food to feed the cat. She fell short of explaining which Christmas cards to send. She obviously underestimated just how bloody useless I am.'

'I'm sure that's not true.' Mollie replied gently. 'Besides, I could leave my husband a million notes and he still wouldn't know how to work the washing machine, so I would say you're doing rather well.'

'In that case, let's use this one.' Herbert said, pointing to the Santa card. 'Sod it.'

'So, Vera Holland.' Picking up the card, Mollie began to write and ensured to finish the name with a flick of the pen. 'Anything else you want me to write in here?'

'Stay away from the gin.' Herbert said bluntly. 'And if you're going to buy people gifts from Poundland, make sure you take the damn labels off.'

Looking up from the card, Mollie raised an eyebrow.

'Really?'

'No!' Herbert chuckled and shook his head. 'My Agatha would turn in her grave. Just a simple *Merry Christmas* will suffice.'

Laughing along, Mollie nodded and returned to the card. For a man who had obviously suffered a monumental loss, Herbert Baxter had certainly kept his sense of humour. The traditional flat cap and tweed jacket were just a cover. The grey moustache, wiry eyebrows and wrinkled skin didn't take away from the contagious smile and wicked laughter. After spending a mere ten minutes in his company, Mollie had a feeling that old Herbert was as mischievous now as he was as a young man.

'Thank you for this.' Herbert said suddenly. 'It's not conventional, I know, but it's a great help to me. A huge help, in fact.'

'You're welcome.' Mollie replied, closing the card and popping it into a red envelope. 'It's my pleasure.'

'I did consider cancelling Christmas altogether this year.' Herbert admitted, letting out another sigh. 'Without Agatha, it just seemed rather pointless.'

'I'm sure Agatha wouldn't have wanted that.' Mollie said softly.

'You're right there.' Smoothing out the list of names, Herbert looked at his wedding ring. 'She loved Christmas, which is why I have to learn to love it too. That's why I'm here today. If it wasn't for this place, I would be sitting on my own feeling sorry for myself right now.'

Twirling the pen around her fingers, Mollie blocked out the sounds around her and focused on Herbert's story.

'When I got a knock at the door a few weeks back, I considered ignoring it. After all, I'd ignored every caller who had taken the trouble to visit. But for one reason or another, I decided to answer it. Lydia, that's the charity representative who visited me, she took control of everything, and I couldn't be more grateful. She arranged for a young man to come and put my decorations up, she booked a place for me on the charity's turkey and tinsel trip, and she invited me here today to give me a hand with these cards.'

Mollie offered him a sympathetic smile as an emotional Herbert paused for breath.

'I'm slowly learning that Christmas is going to be a little different this year.' He continued, raising his wedding ring to his lips and kissing it gently. 'Not quite like the Christmases I have had before, but it will be Christmas all the same, and I am grateful that I have been blessed with another one.'

A lump formed in Mollie's throat and she desperately tried to swallow it. Her mind jumped to her no-Christmas Christmas and she felt a wave of guilt cause her stomach to flip. Seemingly reading Mollie's mind, Herbert peered at her over the rim of his thick glasses.

'You don't get many Christmases on this planet, which is why you should treasure each and every one.' He said wisely. 'Having just one day of the year to remind us how lovely it is to put someone else before ourselves is more important than most people realise until it's too late.'

Feeling tears prick at the corner of her eyes, Mollie nodded and pulled another card towards her.

'Enjoy it, cherish it, but whatever you do, Mollie, *don't* waste it...'

Chapter Seventeen

'Mollie, I thought you said it would be empty...'

Standing in the middle of the crowded car park, Mollie gulped as she looked at the hectic supermarket. Swarms of people rushed in and out of the building, each one pushing a trolley that was brimming with goodies. It was eleven o'clock at night on the twenty-third day of December, and Mollie had come up with the rather ingenious idea of tackling the Christmas food shop in an attempt to beat the crowds. The only problem with Mollie's otherwise fool-proof plan was that everyone else in a three-mile radius had obviously had the same brainwave.

'Let's come back another day.' Max grumbled, turning to leave. 'It's far too late to be fighting over parsnips and stuffing balls.'

'We can't come back another day, Max!' Mollie exclaimed, grabbing the sleeve of his coat. 'Tomorrow is Christmas Eve.'

'Mollie, just look at this place!' He protested. 'You would think they were giving out free iPhones in there!'

Casting the frenzied building a cursory glance, Mollie silently groaned.

'I'm afraid we're just going to have to grin and bear it.' She trilled, hoping her optimistic tone of voice would be enough to encourage Max to put on his big-boy pants and brave the crowds. 'I promised Tim a turkey and a turkey is what he shall get.'

Complaining like a teenager who was being forced to visit his grandparents, Max begrudgingly allowed Mollie to drag him across the congested car park. Headlights from the many waiting cars lit the path in front of them as they headed towards the trolley station. Fumbling around in her purse, Mollie passed a pound coin to Max and signalled for him to get a trolley while she scoured her handbag for the shopping list.

'Houston, we have a problem.' Max announced, tapping

Mollie on the arm to get her attention.

Turning to look at the empty trolley bay, Mollie stamped her foot in frustration. The usually full trolley station was completely empty, and in place of the waiting trolleys was a growing queue of impatient people.

'The supermarket closes in an hour!' Mollie groaned. 'We don't have the time to be waiting around for a trolley!'

'Well, unless you want me to carry everything on my back like a damn donkey, we're going to have to wait like everyone else.' Max replied, joining the end of the queue and pulling up his hood. 'If you can't beat them, join them.'

Not willing to concede defeat so easily, Mollie folded her arms and looked around the bustling car park. Spotting a random shopper loading up his boot, she brushed her damp hair out of her face and sprinted over to him.

'Excuse me...' Mollie said, placing a hand on the trolley she so desperately wanted. 'Are you finished with this?'

'Almost.' Lifting the last case of wine into his car, the perturbed man gave Mollie a cautious glance.

'Amarone.' She remarked. 'Very nice.'

The gilet-wearing man closed his boot and pulled the trolley towards him.

'Can I help you with something?' He asked, fishing his car keys out of his pocket.

'I just thought I would be a good citizen and save you the walk back to the trolley station.' Flashing him her most innocent smile, Mollie reached for the trolley once more. 'Call it my good deed for the day.'

The man shifted his eyes to the line of waiting people and shook his head.

'I think I can manage.' He said, starting to walk away. 'Thanks all the same.'

Quickly blocking his view, Mollie grabbed her purse and held out a fiver.

'Honestly, it's no trouble.' She insisted, holding out the note. 'Here, I think you dropped this.'

Raising his eyebrows, the man laughed and brushed past Mollie with the invaluable trolley.

'Ten!' Mollie shouted, her voice sounding far shriller than

she intended.

'Twenty.' The man demanded, not missing a beat.

Hearing footsteps behind her, Mollie grabbed a twenty from her purse and shoved it towards him. After holding the note up to the moonlight, the man released the trolley and dashed back to the safety of his car.

'Mollie?' Max said, tapping her on the shoulder. 'What's going on?'

'Nothing.' Turning around, Mollie smiled proudly and led the way to the entrance. 'Let's go.'

Struggling to keep up with Mollie's haphazard attempts at a rushed walk, Max looked over his shoulder and gulped.

'I don't know how you managed that, Mollie, and I don't want to.' He said hurriedly. 'But there is a mob of very angry people pointing in our direction, so I think we should pick up the pace.'

Increasing her scurried walk to a rather comical jog, Mollie fought against the urge to look back and navigated her way inside the supermarket.

'Okay. We're going to have to tackle this head-on if we have any hope of getting out of here alive.' She said, whipping her shopping list out of her pocket. 'This is not an undertaking for the faint-hearted.'

Diving out of the way to avoid being run over by a particularly eager shopper who was pushing a pram piled high with bottles of brandy, Mollie waited for Max to respond.

'Max?' She said, giving him a nudge when she realised he was watching a couple of women wrestle over a sack of King Edward potatoes. 'Are you listening? This requires your full attention!'

Tearing his eyes away from the soon-to-be UFC fight, Max clapped his hands together and jumped up and down on the spot like a boxer who was waiting to step into the ring.

'Alright!' He said, taking a peek at the shopping list. 'What's the plan?'

'Here's what we're going to do...' Pulling him towards her, Mollie tried to channel her inner football manager. 'I'm going to read out an item and you're going to go and get it. We need to move fast and we need to move quick. Do you have any questions?'

'Don't *fast* and *quick* mean the same thing?' Max asked, mimicking her authoritative voice.

Mollie responded with a glare and slowly counted to ten.

'Do you have any *sensible* questions?' She repeated, narrowing her eyes.

'Yes.' Max replied. 'Why am I being sent into the ruckus? You're half my size. You could weave in and out of there without anyone even noticing. How about *I'll* read out the list and *you* can retrieve the items?'

'But you're the muscle!' Mollie explained, batting her eyelids and giving his bicep a squeeze. 'It's about time you put all those gym sessions to good work.'

'I suppose I *did* gain a centimetre on my triceps last month.' Flexing his muscles, Max looked down at his arms with pride.

'Does that mean you'll do it?' Mollie asked, waiting to hear the all-important *yes*.

Max responded with a nod as Mollie let out a triumphant cheer. Not wanting to waste a second, she quickly consulted her list.

'We're going to hit the vegetables first.' She instructed. 'Keep your hands up and your head high.'

'Hands up. Head high.' Max repeated. 'Got it.'

Taking a deep breath, Mollie attempted to navigate her ill-gotten trolley through the crush of people.

'Ready?' She asked, positioning the trolley at the head of the vegetable aisle.

'As ready as I'll ever be.' Performing a few quick stretches next to the cauliflower section, Max gave Mollie the nod she was waiting for. 'Hit me with it.'

'Carrots!' She yelled. 'Three bags. Preferably organic.'

Diving into the scrum, Max immediately disappeared amongst the riot of hooded coats as Mollie said a quick prayer that he came back without any major injuries.

'Do they *have* to be organic?' A muffled voice asked.

'Yes!' Mollie replied. 'Actually, just grab whatever you can!'

After a lot of huffing and puffing, Max returned with a number of packets in his arms.

'Two bags of organic. One supermarket own brand.'

'That'll do.' Ticking carrots off her list, Mollie gave Max a high five. 'Next up, broccoli.'

Without needing to be told twice, Max ran back into the scrum faster than Usain Bolt.

'Get the one with the longest expiry date!' She yelled after him.

Hearing a commotion behind her, Mollie looked over her shoulder and watched in horror as a row erupted over the last box of crackers. An angry blonde lady held the box above her head as an equally furious brunette pointed a finger at her accusingly. Sensing all hell was about to break loose, Mollie moved her trolley out of harm's way as Max reappeared.

'One broccoli!' He announced, pushing his way out of the fray and tossing the broccoli into the trolley as though it was a basketball. 'Next?'

'We're going to need more than one bloody broccoli, Max!' Mollie cried. 'Get back in there!'

As Max cursed beneath his breath and returned to the bedlam, Mollie's ears pricked up when she heard a familiar laugh in the distance. Manoeuvring the trolley around the corner, Mollie scanned the crowd in an attempt to pinpoint the voice. Unsurprisingly, the cheese aisle was even more crowded than the rest of the store, meaning that she had more chance of finding a needle in a haystack.

Just as she was about to give up, Mollie spotted her mother at the opposite end of the aisle.

'Mum!' She yelled, cupping her hands around her mouth. *'Mum!'*

Looking up from her position at the deli, Heather Waddles ducked out of view before steering her trolley in the opposite direction. Frowning in confusion, Mollie attempted to chase after her but quickly found herself lost in a hail of trolleys who were also fighting for space.

'Excuse me!' Mollie said, smiling apologetically at her fellow shoppers. 'Can I just squeeze through? Excuse me! Thank you!'

Finally making it to the end of the aisle, Mollie caught a glimpse of her mother's khaki jacket disappearing towards the bakery.

'Mum!' She yelled once more. 'What's going on? Where are you going?'

With her exit blocked by a line of queuing people, Heather slowly turned around and positioned herself in front of her trolley.

'Mollie!' She exclaimed, looking rather guilty indeed. 'What are you doing here?'

'I'm protesting against single-use plastic.' Mollie replied sarcastically. 'I'm doing the Christmas food shop! Why else would I be here at eleven o'clock at night, forty-eight hours before Christmas?'

'But... but I thought you weren't doing a traditional Christmas dinner this year?' Heather stammered, her blue eyes darting around the aisle. 'What happened to your no-Christmas Christmas?'

Running her fingers through her wet hair, Mollie pushed her trolley towards the breadsticks to make room for a new stream of keen shoppers.

'It's a long story that involves a charity, some bribery, a little negotiating and a slice of humble pie.' Mollie admitted. 'But the long and short of it is that we are having a traditional Christmas dinner after all.'

'That's fantastic, Mollie!' Performing a bizarre stretching manoeuvre over her head, Heather grinned manically. 'You know how supportive we have been of your no-Christmas Christmas, but your father will be delighted to know that he will be tucking into a turkey.'

Pulling her brow into a frown, Mollie looked over her shoulder to see who her mother was waving at.

'Just don't forget his mint sauce!' Heather jabbered, brushing her wispy fringe out of her eyes. 'You know how much he loves to have a turkey sandwich before bed. Oh, and cranberry sauce! Colman's. It has to be Colman's...'

'Mum?' Mollie interrupted, suddenly worrying about her mother's state of mind. 'Are you okay?'

'I'm fine!' Heather's strangled voice rang out around the aisle as she pulled the sleeves of her coat over her hands. 'I'm just really excited to celebrate Christmas with you, that's all.'

Coming to the conclusion that her mother had been hitting

the Baileys, Mollie shook her head.

'Anyway, what are you doing here at this time of night?' Mollie asked. 'Isn't it past your bedtime?'

'Err...' Desperately scanning the shelves, Heather grabbed the nearest thing she could reach and studied the label. 'Pistachio nuts! I am here for pistachio nuts.'

'Pistachio nuts?' Mollie repeated.

'Random, isn't it?' Heather threw her head back and laughed, causing her dangly earrings to chime together. 'I saw a man eating a bag of them on the Tube earlier and I just could not stop thinking about bloody pistachio nuts.'

'Right...' Mollie replied dubiously, wondering if she should call her mother's doctor. 'And?'

'And I just *had* to come out and get them! If I didn't know any better, I would believe I was pregnant!' Heather continued to laugh and stopped when she realised Mollie looked completely horrified. 'Don't worry, Mollie, I can assure you that I most certainly am not.'

Trying not to vomit, Mollie grimaced and screwed up her nose in disgust.

'It would have to be the immaculate conception.' Heather continued. 'Let's put it that way.'

'Mum, just stop talking.' Mollie demanded, covering her eyes with her hands. 'Please stop talking.'

Slowly putting the pistachio nuts back onto the shelf, Heather looked down at the ground guiltily.

'Why are you really here, Mum?' Taking a step towards her mother, Mollie folded her arms. 'What's going on?'

Before Mollie could get any closer to her trolley, Heather discreetly attempted to push it away. Within a matter of seconds, an almighty crash caused the busy aisle to fall into silence.

'What the...' Following the bang, Mollie walked down the aisle to discover a display of mince pies scattered across the floor. 'Mum, is this your trolley?'

Looking at the offending trolley that was in the middle of the chaos, Heather gulped as Lawrence appeared with an enormous tin of Roses.

'The Quality Street have sold out, so we will have to settle for Roses.' He said to Heather, helping the flustered shop assistant to pick up the mince pies. 'Don't worry, we're not going to run dry. We've still got those Terry's Chocolate Oranges from Jacqueline.'

'Lawrence!' Heather hissed, her cheeks burning furiously. 'Look who I bumped into!'

Pushing his glasses up the bridge of his nose, Lawrence zoned in on Mollie for the first time.

'Mollie!' He shouted, pushing the trolley away in the same way Heather did. 'What... what are you doing here?'

Grabbing the trolley before it could cause any more damage, Mollie peered at the contents to see what they were so keen on hiding. The trolley was brimming with everything from gammon steaks and smoked salmon to pavlova and trifle, indicating that Mollie's parents were going to throw themselves the Christmas to beat all Christmases.

'Wow.' Mollie commented, picking up a slab of Stilton and holding it out for their inspection. 'Someone is going to let their hair down!'

Realising they both looked more sheepish than when she discovered them lacing their coffees with brandy at a parent-teacher meeting, Mollie dropped the giant block of cheese back into the trolley.

'What is going on with you two?' She asked. 'I'm around five seconds away from having mum sectioned, so one of you better start talking.'

Exchanging wary looks, Heather and Lawrence hung their heads in shame.

'We're sorry, Mollie.' Lawrence said suddenly. 'We really tried to get on board with your no-Christmas Christmas, but as the day drew closer we just felt a little, I don't know, *sad* that we weren't celebrating.'

'Sad?' Mollie repeated, her heart sinking in her chest.

'We're weak, Mollie, okay?' Heather cried, walking over to the trolley and pulling it towards her protectively. 'We need the stuff! We need buttered croissants for breakfast. We need to decorate a Christmas tree and see stockings hanging over the fireplace. We need the house to smell of a roasting turkey, and to see steam rising out of Grandma's gravy boats.'

The sudden passion in her mother's voice caused Mollie to feel a rush of remorse as she looked at her parents' crestfallen faces.

'We need to see your face light up when you tear the wrapping paper off the gifts we know you're going to love.' Heather continued timidly. 'We need cheese and port at midnight, and to fall asleep feeling nauseous because we've eaten far too much chocolate.'

'I suppose we could do without the chocolate nausea, but for us, it just isn't Christmas without all the bells and whistles that come with it.' Lawrence added. 'Sorry, Mollie.'

For the first time, the effects of her enforced no-Christmas Christmas hit home for Mollie. In her attempt to remind everyone that the meaning of Christmas extended to more than what was put on the table, she had inadvertently tipped the scales in the opposite direction. So much so, Mollie's friends and family had gone to the extremes of hiding their festive activities from her as though she was Ebenezer Scrooge himself.

'I never meant to ruin Christmas for you.' Mollie replied, feeling incredibly foolish. 'I simply wanted to make everyone realise that Christmas is about more than this...'

Mollie motioned to the packed trolley as Heather wrapped an arm around her shoulders.

'But you did, Mollie.' Heather said reassuringly. 'Because of you, we actually stopped to think about why we do what we do at Christmas rather than just doing it on autopilot. If your goal was to make us grateful for all of this, you've achieved it in buckets.'

'Really?' Mollie asked, looking at her dad for confirmation this was true.

'I can safely say that I've never been more grateful to see an overflowing trolley in all my life.' Enveloping both Mollie and Heather in a group hug, Lawrence held them tightly. 'Merry Christmas, my darlings.'

As the three of them embraced one another warmly, the sound of laboured breathing caused them to turn around.

'Max!' Mollie exclaimed, her jaw dropping open. 'What the...'

Panting for breath, Max held out a rather bruised broccoli before sliding down to the floor. His hair was in disarray, his clothes were torn and he had what appeared to be the start of a black eye, but for some reason, he still had a silly smile on his face.

'I think I might have broken my ankle, and I definitely took a left hook from an eight-year-old, but I did it.' He announced triumphantly. 'I got the last broccoli..'

Chapter Eighteen

It was the night before Christmas and all was quiet in the McQueen house. Despite her insistence on throwing the perfect no-Christmas Christmas, Mollie found herself enjoying quite the traditional Christmas Eve indeed. Her kitchen cabinets were filled with classic festive treats, Elvis was snoozing in front of the flickering fire, and the Christmas candle that Max had insisted on lighting was filling the living room. If Mollie closed her eyes, she would have truly believed that she was enjoying a nutmeg latte in a snowy alpine forest.

The real irony in how Mollie's Christmas Eve had panned out was that she was really enjoying herself. Love Actually was playing on the television, a tin of Quality Street was on the coffee table, and a toasty Max was stretched out next to her. The tree they decorated was sitting pretty in the window, and the many homemade gifts she wrapped last night were surrounding it. Her rather unusual choice of using last week's newspaper as gift wrap had worked out quite well. Combined with the gold pen she had used to scrawl out each recipient's name, the newspaper could have easily passed for a quirky purchase from Camden Market.

Smiling happily, Mollie dipped her hand into the tin of Quality Street and plucked out a chocolate at random. Her decision to stick with her DIY gifts had given her another reason to smile, but the truth was, she didn't really have any other choice. Not only were the shops closed for Christmas, but she was secretly quite proud of her homemade presents. The only person to escape Mollie's quirky gifts was Tiffany. Considering that Elvis had successfully torn the tampon air freshener to pieces, Mollie decided to hop online and purchase her mother-in-law a voucher for a luxury spa in the city.

Tiffany McQueen had always been the most difficult woman on the planet to buy gifts for. If it didn't come in a little turquoise box, Mollie's mother-in-law simply didn't want it, but a Swedish massage at one of London's most prestigious venues was too good for even the ungiftable Tiff to turn her nose up at.

'Are there any purple ones left?' Max asked, holding out his hand for the chocolates.

Shaking her head, Mollie passed him the iconic tin and waited for the inevitable groan.

'Look under the cushion.' She whispered, trying to hide her growing smile.

Max removed his arm from around Mollie's neck and pointed to the fluffy cushion next to him.

'This one?'

Responding with a nod, Mollie watched as Max gently lifted the cushion in question to reveal a secret stash of purple chocolates.

'Merry Christmas!' She sang. 'You didn't really think I had eaten all of your favourites, did you?'

'For a minute there, Mollie, I really did!' Laughing lightly, Max grabbed one of the purple chocolates and popped it into his mouth. 'I was considering calling Santa and telling him not to bother bringing your gifts tomorrow.'

'Well, when you call him, make sure you thank him for bringing yours.' Leaning over to the Christmas tree, Mollie pulled a red gift bag towards her and presented it to Max.

'You do know that it's very bad to open your gifts before midnight, don't you?' Max replied playfully. 'We might end up on the naughty list.'

'I'll take my chances.' Mollie said, smiling brightly. 'Go on. Open it.'

Wiping his hands on his jeans, Max dived into the gift bag and produced a pack of cards.

'Playing cards?' He asked.

'*Promise* cards.' Mollie corrected, encouraging him to open them. 'On the back of each playing card is a promise that you can cash in at your leisure. Fifty-two cards for fifty-two weeks of the year.'

Flipping through the deck, Max turned over cards at random.

'*I promise to let you have control of the television remote.*'

He read aloud. '*I promise not to wake you up when you're snoring*. Are these for real?'

'As real as Santa.' Mollie replied seriously. 'And if you don't believe in Santa, you only deserve socks for Christmas.'

Laughing along, Max continued to read the promises out loud.

'*I promise to at least attempt to cook a homemade meal once a week. I promise to empty the litter tray. I promise to... I promise to never have another no-Christmas Christmas.*'

Pursing his lips, Max studied the card in his hands closely before bringing his eyes up to meet Mollie's.

'You know what?' He said slowly. 'I'm not sure about that last one.'

'You're not?' Mollie replied in surprise. 'Why?'

'Because on one level or another, I believe a no-Christmas Christmas is exactly what we have all needed.' Slipping the playing cards back into their packet, Max positioned the gift bag between him and Mollie. 'It's easy to get carried away at this time of year, and you have made us all think that little bit deeper about what we're all doing. For that, I thank you. It seems the best presents in life don't always come gift-wrapped.'

'Is that a dig at my beautiful wrapping paper?' Mollie asked, cocking her head towards the Christmas tree.

Following Mollie's gaze, Max chuckled at the sight of Mollie's newspaper gift wrap.

'It's actually rather hypocritical of me to be laughing right now.' He said, rolling off the sofa and disappearing into the kitchen. 'It seems great minds think alike.'

Clueless as to what he was talking about, Mollie tapped her foot with intrigue until Max returned holding out a bunch of flowers.

'Now, I couldn't find any dogtooth violets or black-eyed Susans, and I didn't pick these by hand.' He admitted, presenting Mollie with the beautiful bouquet. 'However, I did choose every single flower myself.'

Accepting the bouquet, Mollie smiled as she looked at the incredible collection of freesias, chrysanthemums and eucalyptus.

'You really chose these yourself?' She asked, leaning over the flowers and inhaling deeply. 'You didn't have any help?'

'None at all.' Max said proudly. 'I refused every offer of assistance from the florist and spent no less than two whole hours making my selection, but I must admit to having a little help from Google with the wrapping.'

Taking the flowers out of the box, Mollie giggled when she noticed the stems had been wrapped in newspaper.

'You used newspaper too!' She exclaimed. 'Great minds really do think alike!'

'Not just any old newspaper.' Looking rather pleased with himself, Max grinned from ear to ear. 'Take a look at the date.'

Mollie followed his instructions and gasped when she spotted the date stamp.

'Is this?'

'That is a newspaper from the day we met.' He confirmed. 'Not the actual newspaper. I printed a copy off the internet, but you get the sentiment.'

Blown away by Max's thoughtful gesture, Mollie placed the flowers on the coffee table and threw her arms around his neck.

'Max!' She cried. 'This is the most romantic thing you have ever done for me.'

'I'm guessing that you approve?' He asked, between being attacked by a flurry of kisses. 'Did I get it right for once?'

Before Mollie could reply, a loud knock at the door caught their attention.

'It's a bit early for Santa.' Max remarked, removing Mollie's arms from around his neck and glancing at the clock. 'But it's not too early for another old person with a grey beard.'

'I sincerely hope you're not talking about Mrs Heckles.' Stepping into her slippers, Mollie smoothed down her hair and followed Max out of the living room. 'I'll have you know that her chin whiskers are no more since she demanded I attack them with a pair of tweezers. That was a Friday evening I'll never forget.'

'Thanks for that rather frightening image, Mollie.' Max retorted, leading the way down the hallway and shuddering. 'That's an image *I'll* never forget.'

Batting his arm playfully, Mollie looked over Max's shoulder as he pulled open the door to reveal Mrs Heckles. Wearing a coat that resembled a duvet and a woolly scarf large enough to wrap around a small elephant, Mollie's neighbour grinned widely.

'Why, hello there, Mrs Heckles!' Max said, leaning against the wall. 'Go on then. Let's have it.'

Without saying a word, Mrs Heckles raised her fingers to her lips and whistled loudly. Exchanging confused glances with Max, Mollie looked on in wonder as a group of well-dressed people appeared from the shadows and walked up the garden path. Their lanterns lit up the night sky, casting a warm glow around Mrs Heckles as they came to a stop behind her and produced a series of identical red books.

Clapping her hands together excitedly, Mollie huddled next to Max while Mrs Heckles and her army of carollers broke out into a hauntingly beautiful rendition of Silent Night. Tiny snowflakes fell to the ground, creating the perfect backdrop to the idyllic Christmas scene that was unfolding on Mollie's doorstep. Their harmonious voices filled the quiet street, wrapping around the row of houses like a comforting blanket.

As the carollers eventually came to a gentle stop, Mollie and Max erupted into a round of well-earned applause.

'Mrs Heckles!' Mollie cried, clutching her hands to her face. 'That was incredible!'

'It really was.' Max agreed. 'If I squinted, I'd believe you were Katherine Jenkins.'

'Give over.' Mrs Heckles chuckled as her legion of carollers retreated down the path. 'Ten houses down, dozens more to go.'

'What a perfect way to spend Christmas Eve.' Watching the carollers make their way across the snowy street, Mollie sighed wistfully. 'I wish we could join you.'

'You *are* joining us.' Mrs Heckles croaked. 'Get your coat.'

Looking down at her fluffy dressing gown, Mollie glanced at Max's crocodile onesie dubiously.

'I don't think we're really dressed for the occasion.' She explained, motioning to their nightwear.

'So?' A determined Mrs Heckles fired back. 'I thought you

were breaking the rules this year?'

Locking eyes with Max, Mollie waited for the nod of approval before grabbing her duffel coat. The cold air nipped at her bare legs as she quickly exchanged her slippers for a pair of walking boots and waited for Max to zip up his parka.

'Here...' Mrs Heckles said, passing Mollie a red book of her own as she stepped out of the house. 'Merry Christmas, Mollie.'

Taking the carol book, Mollie linked arms with Mrs Heckles while Max locked the door.

'Merry Christmas, Mrs Heckles...'

Chapter Nineteen

'Do I mix the beans in with the mashed potatoes, or are the mashed potatoes added to the beans?' Max asked, wiping his hands on his Rudolph apron. 'It might sound like a trivial question, but for all we know, it could be like the age-old scone debacle. Cream before jam or jam before cream?'

Joining Max at the kitchen island, Mollie peered into the bowl of mashed potatoes and reached into her pocket for her mobile phone.

'If I remember correctly, Tim was quite clear about this.' She replied, quickly bringing up the text message which outlined his mother's famous recipe. 'Here we go... *The beans are preheated on the hob and then added to the mashed potatoes.* Tim goes on to say that in order to create the perfect balance, it should be exactly half a tin of beans per two servings of mashed potato.'

'Half a tin of beans per two servings of mashed potato.' Max repeated. 'Got it.'

Placing her phone on the counter, Mollie sang along to the radio as Max carefully measured out the baked beans. Smells that only existed on December twenty-fifth filled the kitchen, encouraging Mollie to stick her finger into the bowl of creamy mashed potatoes.

'I bet you didn't expect to be cracking open tins of beans on Christmas Day, did you?' She joked, pulling her mimosa towards her. 'They're not exactly up there with croissants and profiteroles.'

Dropping numerous empty packets into the recycling bin, Max tossed a tea towel over his shoulder and clinked his glass against Mollie's.

'To be quite honest, Mollie, after your no-Christmas Christmas plans, I'm just relieved to be cooking a Christmas dinner at all.' He replied, leaning over the kitchen island and planting a kiss on Mollie's lips. 'Now get out of my kitchen.'

'You don't want my help?' Mollie gasped. 'I'm mightily offended.'

'Considering that you have a tendency to burn things simply by looking at them, and the fact that you've spent the entire morning stealing the food I am trying to prepare, I'm going to respectfully decline your offer.' Checking the timer on the oven, Max shooed Mollie away. 'But your willingness to help has been duly noted.'

Unable to resist another taste of Max's mashed potatoes, Mollie stuck her finger into the bowl for a final time before racing into the living room. The warmth from the radiators heated the cosy room as she collapsed onto the sofa and sighed happily. It was shortly before one o'clock in the afternoon, which meant that Mollie would usually be wafting a pair of oven gloves under the fire alarm while Max juggled ten kitchen appliances in the battle to serve everything on time. However, unlike the Christmases they had thrown in the past, Mollie found herself to be completely at ease.

This year, for whatever reason, things appeared to be going without so much as a hiccup. Max didn't have numerous plasters stuck to his fingers, Mollie wasn't knocking on neighbours' doors in a desperate bid to borrow an Oxo cube, and unfortunately for the robins in the garden, they weren't feasting on burnt carrots. As such, Mollie didn't really know what to do with herself. The table had been laid, the gifts had been wrapped, and she and Max were rocking their favourite Christmas jumpers. With all the boxes ticked, all there was left for Mollie to do was sit back and wait for her guests to arrive.

After flicking through the television channels, she wandered across the rug and peered out of the window. The usually quiet street was alive with the quintessential charm of Christmas. A bunch of children whom Mollie didn't recognise were attempting to build a snowman out of the piles of slush that remained from yesterday's snowfall, a smartly dressed couple laughed merrily as they made their way to the pub for a festive drink or two, and numerous cars were crawling along the road on the journey to visit loved ones.

Fixing her gaze on a silver vehicle that had pulled up on the opposite side of the street, Mollie watched as the doors opened and an elderly gentleman stepped out onto the pavement. Waving his hands above his head, the man beamed brightly as the group of children abandoned their snowman and ran over to him with open arms. Their joyous cheers warmed the cold air as they enveloped him in a hug.

Finally managing to prise himself away from the many eager pairs of arms, the man pointed to the passenger seat of the car and the children immediately teared over to it. Completely oblivious to the realisation that their Christmas reunion was being watched, a beautiful lady stepped out of the car and presented the children with a pile of gifts. Unable to contain their excitement, they jumped up and down on the spot as who Mollie presumed were their grandparents motioned for them to go inside the house before opening them.

As she lost herself in the Christmas cheer that was taking place outside of her window, Mollie was distracted by a rather authoritative knocking at the door.

'Mollie?' Max yelled from the kitchen. 'Can you get that?'

'I'm on it!' She replied, smoothing down her hair as she rushed to the front door. 'Three guesses as to who it is?'

'Considering it is one o'clock exactly, I am going to go with our friendly neighbourhood heckler?'

'And you would be correct... *Hello, Mrs Heckles!*' Mollie exclaimed, loud enough for Max to hear as she pulled open the door. 'Merry Christmas!'

'Merry Christmas!' Mrs Heckles hollered, holding out a gift box. 'This is for you!'

'Oh, Mrs Heckles!' Graciously accepting the silver box, Mollie peeked inside and quickly closed it when Mrs Heckles hit her with her walking stick. 'Ouch!'

'Don't open it out here!' Mrs Heckles cried. 'Let us in there!'

'Us?' Mollie repeated, stepping aside to allow Mrs Heckles room to step into the hallway.

'Yeah, I invited Frankie to come along.' Bustling her way into the house, Mrs Heckles paused to admire the many Christmas cards that Mollie had stuck to the bannister with the help of a bumper pack of Blu Tack. 'That's alright, isn't it? He was only going to spend the day wallowing in his own pity.'

Usually, notification of an unexpected guest would have sent Mollie into a meltdown, but unbeknown to Mrs Heckles, Frankie already had a seat waiting for him around the dining table. You see, Mollie had known Mrs Heckles for long enough to know that she would more than likely bring old Frankie along. Despite constantly playing down her involvement with Frankie, Mollie was very aware that Mrs Heckles was growing rather fond of her ex-nemesis. Being as stubborn as she was grey, Mrs Heckles would rather give up her veneers than admit wanting to spend Christmas with him.

'Of course it's alright.' Mollie replied. 'Come on in, Frankie.'

'Hi, Megan!' He cheered, carrying Misty's crate into the house. 'Happy Christmas!'

'For the love of cats and dogs, Frankie!' Mrs Heckles cackled, giving him a whack with her walking stick. 'Her name is Mollie, not bloody Megan!'

Blinking back at Mrs Heckles blankly, Frankie turned to look at Mollie.

'Is it?' He asked, scratching his head.

Feeling her cheeks flush, Mollie nodded and politely closed the door behind him.

'Oh, well I'm sorry about that, Mollie.' Frankie said, laughing to himself. 'Happy Christmas anyway.'

'Merry Christmas, Frankie.' Mollie replied. 'It's great to have you with us.'

Groaning as he bent down to let Misty out of her crate, Frankie yanked his hand away when Misty took a well-aimed swipe at his fingers.

'She's getting a little feisty in her mature years!' Mollie remarked, watched Misty bolt out of her crate in search of Elvis. 'She must be taking tips from her owner.'

'I heard that!' Mrs Heckles yelled over her shoulder. 'But luckily for you it's Christmas, and absolutely *nothing* could make me mad today.'

Sharing an amused smile with Frankie, Mollie followed Mrs Heckles through the house as she shuffled into the kitchen to greet Max.

'Something smells good in here!' Mrs Heckles commented, hobbling over to Max and throwing her arms around him. 'I haven't heard any fire alarms blaring, so I'm guessing Mollie hasn't been in here much today?'

'You know her too well!' Max chuckled. 'Merry Christmas, Mrs Heckles.'

'Merry Christmas, Max.' Mrs Heckles replied, planting a pastel pink kiss on his cheek. 'This is for you...'

'Is it a football?' He joked, accepting the bottle-shaped gift and placing it next to the sink.

'How did you guess?' Throwing her head back, Mrs Heckles laughed and nudged Max in jest. 'That's the good stuff. Feel free to crack it open.'

'I'm one step ahead, Mrs Heckles!' Already grabbing four glasses from the cupboard, Max smiled gratefully. 'And thank you.'

'That's my boy!' Mrs Heckle said happily, before turning back to Mollie. 'Right, where do you want us?'

'If you would like to follow me into the living room, I have arranged a selection of appetisers for us to enjoy before dinner...' Mollie's voice trailed off as Frankie dashed out of the kitchen at hearing the word *appetisers*.

'Is he hungry?' Max asked, opening the bottle of fizz with a pop.

'He's always bloody hungry.' Mrs Heckles muttered. 'He ate three tins of Spam for supper last night. He's got hollow legs.'

Stifling a giggle, Mollie led the way into the living room and found Frankie tucking into the salmon blinis as both cats looked on with hungry eyes.

'Gannet.' Mrs Heckles mumbled, taking a seat next to him on the sofa.

'Hey, it's Christmas!' Stuffing another blini into his mouth, Frankie loaded up a napkin with devilled eggs. 'It's the one time of year when you're allowed to overeat. Right, Megan?'

'Mollie.' Mrs Heckles corrected sharply.

'Sorry, Mollie.'

'You knock yourself out, Frankie.' Mollie replied. 'Christmas comes but once a year.'

'On that note.' Mrs Heckles interjected, pointing at the gift box that was still in Mollie's hand. 'Pop that under the tree with the others.'

'Don't you want me to open it?' Giving the box a gentle squeeze for a clue as to what was inside, Mollie reached for the lid.

'Let's have a drink first.' Giving Mollie a knowing look, Mrs Heckles patted her arm and pointed to the Christmas tree. 'Go on.'

Filled with intrigue, Mollie did as she was told and placed the glittering box amongst the pile of presents.

'Here we go, guys!' Max said, walking into the living room with two glasses. 'Ladies first.'

Accepting a flute of crisp bubbles, Mollie perched on the arm of the sofa next to Mrs Heckles while Max hurried back to the kitchen for the remaining glasses. Once everyone had a flute in their hand, Max raised his own glass in the air and cleared his throat.

'To good friends and happy Christmases!' He declared.

'Good friends and happy Christmases!' Mollie and Mrs Heckles repeated in unison.

'And full bellies!' Frankie managed, between shovelling yet more canapes into his mouth.

As everyone clinked their glasses together, Mollie laughed and pushed the tray of blinis towards Frankie.

'And full bellies, Frankie.' She agreed. '*Always* full bellies...'

Chapter Twenty

The sound of joyous laughter filled the crowded dining room as Mollie took her seat opposite Max at the head of the table and smiled happily. With thirteen people crammed around the dining table, it was safe to say that it was more than a little congested, but it didn't matter one jot. If anything, the rather haphazard seating arrangements only added to the charm. There was little elbow room, and a fair amount of accidental nudging was taking place, but Mollie wouldn't change it for all the gifts in Lapland.

Mrs Heckles and Frankie were tucking into their parsnip soup, Margot and Jasper were stealing one another's bread rolls, the two sets of parents were animatedly sharing tips on how to roast the perfect bird, Tim was passing around bottles of his homemade cider, and Eugenie was laughing hysterically as a rather tipsy Kenny stuck breadsticks up his nostrils. It wasn't a scene out of Nigella's Christmas Kitchen, but it was everything Mollie had wanted and more.

Raising her glass to her lips, Mollie laughed as she watched Elvis fire across the rug with Misty hot on his furry heels. Despite her no-Christmas Christmas plans going out of the window, Mollie had inadvertently got her way with one of her no-Christmas demands. In a change from all the Christmases Mollie had lived through before, the pile of gifts remained untouched beneath the Christmas tree.

Ever since she was a young girl, Mollie McQueen had raced down the stairs on Christmas Day the very second she peeled open her eyes. The anticipation of tearing off the wrapping paper in a bid to discover what fabulous gift was waiting for her inside had always been too strong for her to ignore. This year, however, not a single present had been touched. In her bid to recapture the true essence of Christmas, Mollie had followed Mrs Heckles' lead and instructed every guest who stepped over the threshold to place their gifts under the tree.

As such, Mollie and the gang had enjoyed hours of meaningful conversation without giving a second thought to what Santa had graced them with, which is exactly what she had wanted to accomplish.

Feeling rather pleased with herself, Mollie attempted to join in with one of the many spirited conversations that were taking place around the table.

'So, you just help for free?' Tiffany asked Eugenie, swirling Champagne around her glass. 'There's no form of payment?'

Realising that Eugenie was bringing Tiffany up to date on their charity work, Mollie looked on with intrigue as Eugenie shook her head in response to Tiff's question.

'You just helped out of the goodness of your hearts?' Tiffany persisted, clearly struggling to understand the concept.

'That's correct.' Eugenie replied. 'The charity is in need of volunteers all year round, so there's still time for you to get involved.'

'I see.' Sipping her Bollinger slowly, Tiffany cocked her head to one side and twirled a diamond earring around her finger. 'I've never really thought about volunteering before. Well, not for anything other than aesthetic procedures and weight-loss trials.'

Hiding her growing smile behind her glass, Mollie shared an amused look with Eugenie. For the past ten minutes, Eugenie had been filling Tiffany in on the volunteer work she and the gang had done for the Rainbow Volunteer Group, but it seemed the idea of doing something nice for someone who could never repay you was completely lost on Tiff.

'Alright!' Max said suddenly, standing up and clapping his hands together. 'Who is ready for the main event?'

A loud cheer rang out around the crowded dining table as Mollie pushed out her chair to give Max a helping hand in the kitchen.

'How was that, Mrs Heckles?' She asked, whipping away her empty dish.

'Fabulous!' Mrs Heckles replied. 'Like Christmas in a bowl!'

Nodding in response, Mollie moved along to Frankie.

'That was fantastic.' He gushed, attempting to mop up the last smear of soup before Mollie could remove the bowl from his grasp. 'There's nothing like homemade soup, is there? I should know, I once worked at The Fat Swan. You can't fool me with any shop-bought slop. Give my compliments to the chef.'

Being very aware that the soup in question came out of a Waitrose tin, Mollie smiled politely and continued to gather the remaining dishes before joining Max in the kitchen.

'How are we getting on in here?' She asked, placing the used bowls into the dishwasher. 'Anything I can do to help?'

Carefully placing Chantenay carrots onto the line of waiting plates, Max wiped a bead of sweat off his forehead.

'I don't want to speak too soon, Mollie, but I *think* I have everything under control...' Max's voice tapered off as a trail of smoke made its way towards the fire alarm.

Jumping into action, Mollie swiftly removed the offending tray from the oven and opened the kitchen window in an attempt to clear the air.

'The stuffing!' Max shrieked, shutting the door to the dining room with his hip. 'I completely forgot about the stuffing! You've just saved my bacon!'

'So, I've finally been of some use in the kitchen.' Reaching for a tea towel, Mollie leaned against the sink and smirked. 'Is that what you're saying?'

'I think I am!' Inspecting the stuffing closely, Max breathed a sigh of relief upon realising Mollie had rescued the essential component just in time. 'It's a Christmas miracle!'

'Another one?' Mollie said, spraying her Secret Santa room spray around the kitchen. 'I've heard that phrase quite a lot lately.'

'Then you're very, *very* lucky.' Taking the tea towel from her, Max wiped a tiny smear of soup off Mollie's cheek. 'Some people spend a lifetime waiting for a Christmas miracle.'

'We've got our friends and family around us, scrumptious food to eat and a lovely home to enjoy it in. We're very lucky indeed.' She agreed, standing on the tips of her toes to kiss him. 'Merry Christmas, Max.'

'Merry Christmas.' Max's grey eyes crinkled into his smile as he stared back at Mollie and winked. 'Now get...'

'Out of your kitchen.' She finished for him. 'I know.'

Leaving him to plate the food, Mollie grabbed another bottle of wine from the fridge and returned to their guests. Having a dining room that was alive with laughter and joy made her heart swell as she scanned the table in search of a glass that required refilling. Confident that everyone had a suitable drink in their hand, Mollie started to retreat to her seat when her gaze landed on the one empty chair between Eugenie and Tim. Her eyes flicked to the clock on the wall and she let out a sigh as Max entered the room with the first of the plates.

'This looks amazing!' Ralph gushed, clapping Max on the back. 'Considering that you couldn't even touch a piece of meat last year, you've really outdone yourself. Well done, son. Three cheers for the chef!'

'*Hip hip hooray!*'

As the group exploded into enthusiastic chatter once again, Mollie jumped up when she heard a gentle knock at the door. Quietly excusing herself, she walked over to the window and peered outside. A set of footsteps in the sludge indicated that another visitor had arrived, but the falling sleet made it impossible to see who.

Heading down the hallway, Mollie dusted down her blouse before pulling open the door.

'Joyce!' She exclaimed. 'You came!'

Shifting her weight from one foot to the other, the Payne and Carter receptionist looked at Mollie nervously and held out a glass bottle.

'The invite didn't specify what to bring, so I brought gin.' She said glumly, raising her lips into a hesitant smile. 'Mother's ruin. Always good to have on hand at this time of year.'

'Thank you, Joyce.' Accepting the bottle, Mollie beckoned for her to come inside. 'You didn't have to bring anything. Just having you with us is enough.'

'I'm glad to hear it because I didn't bring you anything else.' Joyce replied bluntly, brushing a small pile of sleet off her sleeve.

Slightly taken aback, Mollie smiled thinly and wondered if she had made a mistake in inviting Joyce to spend Christmas with them.

'I'm kidding.' Joyce said suddenly, smiling genuinely for the first time as she held out a black box. 'That was a joke. Happy Christmas.'

Laughing with relief, Mollie accepted the box and gave her a brief hug.

'I'll pop this under the tree with the others.' She said gratefully. 'Come on, let me introduce you to everyone.'

As Mollie retraced her steps along the hallway, she stopped when she realised that Joyce wasn't following her.

'Is everything okay?' She asked, pausing with her hand on the dining room door. 'Joyce?'

Twiddling her thumbs anxiously, Joyce opened and closed her mouth repeatedly.

'Mollie, I just want to let you know that this is the nicest thing anyone has ever done for me.' She mumbled, refusing to look Mollie in the eye. 'So, thank you.'

'Oh, Joyce! There's really no need to...'

Mollie's voice trailed off as Joyce took a few cautious steps forwards before throwing her arms around Mollie's neck.

Completely touched by Joyce's unusual display of affection, Mollie relaxed her posture and hugged the grouchy receptionist back.

'Let's get you a drink.' Mollie said warmly, finally releasing Joyce. 'Shall we?'

After being given the nod of approval to go ahead, Mollie pushed open the door to the dining room and cleared her throat. Right on cue, the room fell into silence as everyone turned to look at Mollie and the mystery guest.

'Everyone, this is my colleague, Joyce.' Mollie said, gently pulling Joyce into view. 'She's a little late to the party, but I would like you all to make her feel very welcome.'

True to form, the group immediately set to work at inviting Joyce into their merry clique.

'Happy Christmas, Joyce!'

'Hi, Joyce!'

'Welcome to the McQueen house!'

As of chorus of encouraging introductions took place, Mollie smiled with pride at her friends and family. Welcoming a stranger into their Christmas celebrations most likely wasn't on their to-do list, but the eccentric bunch of lovely people surrounding Mollie's dining table accepted Joyce like she was one of their own.

'Merry Christmas, Joyce!' Tim said, raising his bottle of cider in the air and tapping the empty chair next to him. 'Get yourself over here!'

Without an ounce of the hesitation that she displayed outside, Joyce hotfooted her way over to Tim and took a seat in one of the many chairs that Mollie had borrowed from Mrs Heckles.

'What can I get you to drink, Joyce?' Mollie asked, motioning to the selection of bottles in the middle of the table. 'I have red, white, a nice bottle of bubbles...'

'You could try my homemade cider?' Tim offered.

'Or you could try Tim's homemade cider.' Mollie repeated. 'What's it going to be?'

'I think I'll try the cider.' Accepting a bottle from Tim, Joyce gave him a tight-lipped smile as he struggled to remove the lid. 'Do you really make this yourself?'

'I do. Well, I *did*.' Tim replied, finally removing the lid and accidentally firing it into Kenny's glass in the process. 'I used to have a microbrewery in my mum's spare room, but my new place doesn't have the luxury of a spare room, or any spare space at all, actually.'

'You could make it in the bathtub.' Joyce joked.

'I *could* make it in the bathtub...'

Leaving Joyce to get acquainted with the rest of the group, Mollie deposited her gift beneath the tree as Max placed the final plates onto the dining table.

'Just so you know...' Mollie whispered to Joyce. 'Everything on your plate is completely free of dairy products. Just don't tell the others. What they don't know won't hurt them. Ignorance is bliss.'

Giving Mollie the thumbs-up sign, Joyce draped a napkin across her knee as Max tapped a fork against his glass.

'Okay, guys! I have an announcement to make.' He said excitedly, moving aside in order for Mollie to get back to her seat. 'If you take a closer look at your mashed potatoes, you will notice that Christmas dinner has a slight twist this year.'

Giving his guests a moment to recognise what he was talking about, Max waited for the many intrigued *oohs*.

'Now, I think I speak for all of us when I say that baked beans aren't something usually associated with turkey, but in remembrance of Dottie, Tim made this special request and I was more than happy to oblige.' Looking in Tim's direction, Max took a deep breath. 'Therefore, it is only right that Tim gets the first taste.'

Knowing how much this small gesture meant to Tim, Mollie looked on as he reached for his fork and dived into the mashed potatoes that had broken all the rules of Christmas.

'It's perfect.' Tim announced, causing the group to erupt into yet another round of applause. 'Exactly the right consistency and the perfect ratio of beans to mash. Spot on, M-Dog. Thank you.'

Mollie caught Tim's eye and winked as Max held his glass in the air and encouraged everyone else to do the same.

'To Dottie!' He said fondly. 'The lady who left a little sparkle wherever she went.'

'*To Dottie...*'

Chapter Twenty-One

Placing a hand on her stomach, Mollie yawned lazily and blinked in a bid to focus her tired eyes on the television screen. After consuming more calories than she could count, the usually leisurely task of keeping herself awake seemed like mission impossible. The heat from the fire was coaxing her to claim forty winks, but Mollie was determined to resist.

Looking around the living room, it appeared that the cosy setting had lured more than one guest to the land of nod. Mrs Heckles was snoozing next to Frankie on the sofa, Heather's eyes were closing while she stroked a dozing Elvis, and Ralph was snoring lightly next to a rather unimpressed Tiffany. However, not everyone had been seduced by the temptation of the roaring flames. Tim was having a heated debate with Lawrence about the best Christmas movies, Margot and Jasper were curled up in the armchair playing a game of silent charades, and Kenny had finally succumbed to joining Joyce and Max in a rather tipsy rendition of Fairytale of New York.

Turning back to the television, Mollie smiled and cradled her glass against her chest. It's a Wonderful Life had forever been her favourite Christmas film, and as the years drifted by, her love for it continued to grow. A post-dinner glass of port while watching the famous movie was a Christmas tradition that Mollie had taken over from her grandmother, and she didn't plan on changing it anytime soon.

Sitting cross-legged on the carpet, watching the credits to the iconic movie roll, Mollie was satisfied that she had thrown the perfect Christmas. Bellies were full, faces were smiling, and the gifts had *still* not been opened. As Mollie's eyes flicked to the pile of gifts under the tree, she felt a swell of pride. Too busy enjoying the day, not a single person had opened a single present. The impressive display of gifts remained untouched. Without Mollie needing to nag them to cherish the true meaning of Christmas, each and every one of her guests had done exactly that. After a few wrong turns along the way, Mollie McQueen had pulled off her no-Christmas Christmas without even realising it, which just made it all the more satisfying.

'Guys?' She said, turning down the volume on the television and addressing her guests. 'We haven't opened the gifts!'

Springing to life, Mrs Heckles sat up straight and rubbed her hands together.

'Well, what are you waiting for?' She asked, pointing towards the Christmas tree with the end of her walking stick. 'The day is nearly over! Crack them open!'

A buzz passed around the room as Mollie walked over to the tree and grabbed as many gifts as she could carry.

'Margot, this one's for you.' She said, studying the handwritten label. 'Merry Christmas!'

Taking the gift, Margot clapped her hands together excitedly as Mollie continued to distribute the presents.

'Mrs Heckles... Jasper... Tim... Mum... Kenny... Dad....'

Making her way around the living room, allocating gifts and distributing hugs, Mollie smiled at the undeniable sound of wrapping paper being torn apart.

'Oh, thank you, Mollie!' Heather exclaimed, holding up the paperclip earrings that Mollie had made earlier in the month. 'These are fantastic!'

'Do you really like them?' Mollie asked. 'I made them myself.'

'Of course I do.' Slipping the earrings into her ears, Heather turned her head from left to right to show off her unusual gift. 'What do you think? Do they suit me?'

'They really do!' Eugenie gushed, nodding approvingly. 'Stationary jewellery is very in vogue this season.'

Being very aware that stationary jewellery was nothing more than a term that Eugenie had pulled out of thin air, Mollie gave her a grateful wink.

'Thank you, Mollie.' Squeezing her daughter tightly, Heather ironed out the newspaper and placed it next to her feet. 'Merry Christmas, my love.'

'Merry Christmas, Mum.'

'Mollie, this is amazing!' Margot squealed, applying a slick of the Vaseline to her lips and running over to the mirror. 'You know that I've been looking for a new lip balm! How did you get the colour so perfect?'

Thanking her lucky stars that her DIY gifts had been so well received, Mollie simply shrugged bashfully as the sound of Mrs Heckles' familiar cackle caught her attention.

'What the hell is this?' Mrs Heckles asked, holding up the white box in confusion.

'It's tooth whitening paste.' Mollie explained. 'It's made solely from natural ingredients, so it won't damage your veneers. Now you can whiten to your heart's content.'

Quietly impressed, Mrs Heckles raised a grey eyebrow and gave it the nod of approval.

'How did you know this is exactly what I asked Santa for?' She demanded, placing the whitening powder into the safety of her handbag. 'You got some reindeers out the back?'

'I have a secret line to the North Pole.' Bending down to give her neighbour a hug, Mollie smiled as Mrs Heckles patted her on the back. 'Merry Christmas, Mrs Heckles.'

'A DVD?' Lawrence said, turning the CD over in his hands.

'It's actually a CD, Dad.' Slipping her hands into the pockets of her hoody, Mollie joined her dad on the sofa. 'There should be a song list in the envelope.'

Tipping the envelope upside down, Lawrence grabbed the handwritten list before it fell to the floor.

'The Beautiful South *and* The Proclaimers?' He cheered. 'Did you put this together yourself?'

Mollie nodded and grinned from ear to ear. After questioning how well her homemade gifts would go down, it seemed that her hesitations were completely unjustified. Everyone appeared to be genuinely loving their presents. Mollie had made it her mission to prove that it was the thought that counted, and judging by the many happy faces around her, it appeared that she had done exactly that.

While the rest of the group opened their gifts, Mollie watched as Margot passed Heather another box to open. Recalling the hideous gold tiara Margot foolishly purchased at the Christmas market, Mollie looked on with intrigue.

'Beautiful wrapping, Margot.' Heather remarked. 'As

always.'

Revelling in her mother's compliment, Margot sat up straight as Heather carefully removed the luxury paper to reveal a tiny hemp bag. A red label dangled from a knotted rope that was holding it all together perfectly.

'It's a... Christmas tree!' Heather said animatedly.

'It's a what?' Mollie asked, frowning in confusion.

'A Christmas tree.' Heather repeated, holding up the hemp bag for Mollie to see for herself.

'A grow-your-own Christmas tree, to be precise.' Margot confirmed happily. 'I thought you could put it in Aunt Jacqueline's garden, next to the rose bush we planted in memory of grandma.'

'Margot, that is such a lovely thought.' Looking down at the bag, Heather smiled affectionately. 'Thank you so much.'

'It comes with a complete set of instructions.' Margot explained, pointing to the red tag. 'It sounds fool-proof, to be honest. Although, it does take quite a while to grow. Don't be expecting to hang baubles on it this time next year.'

'With your mother's record of keeping plants alive, we will probably be throwing it on the bonfire come November.' Lawrence chuckled. 'Remember that peace lily Mollie bought us for our anniversary last year? The poor thing turned yellow and died the second it realised your mother intended on giving it enough water to sink a cruise ship.'

'I think you will find that Pascal passed away due to overexposure to sunlight.' Heather corrected, giving Lawrence a stern look. 'I am a woman of many talents, but controlling when the United Kingdom is going to be treated to a heatwave is unfortunately not one of them.'

'Pascal?' Tim laughed and dived into the box of Quality Street that was on the coffee table. 'Do you name all of your plants?'

'I do indeed.' Heather confirmed, without a hint of blush. 'There was Maggie, she was a maidenhair fern. Steve the spider plant. Oh, and I can never forget Charles. Charles was a beautiful cactus. He only had spines on the top of his head. He looked like a little hedgehog. I did consider naming him Bart, you know, from The Simpsons?'

'Do you notice the use of the past tense here?' Lawrence said comically, causing the rest of the group to laugh. 'Sorry, love. I'm sure this will be the one to break the mould. Come on then, what's this one's name?'

As Heather studied the label intently, Mollie tapped Margot on the shoulder.

'What happened to the gold tiara?' She whispered. 'Did you come to your senses?'

'Let's just say that divine intervention played a role.' Looking up at her sister, Margot smiled and raised her glass of port to her lips. '*Does* having a little sister who won't quit waffling on about the true meaning of Christmas count as divine intervention?'

'I'm pretty confident that it does.' Mollie replied, nudging her sister playfully.

'Plus, my credit card statement arrived and the price of that tiara was going to have bailiffs knocking at my door come Boxing Day.' Giggling to herself, Margot rested her head against Mollie's arm. 'I have to admit, the seller wasn't very impressed when I went down there to return it. She must have had a dozen of those bloody tiaras on that stall. The last one, my eye!'

Mollie giggled and looked up as Heather finally settled on a name.

'Carol.' She announced. 'Carol the Christmas tree.'

'I think that deserves a toast, don't you?' Frankie said, holding out his glass. 'To Carol!'

'To Carol!' The group echoed.

Raising her eyebrows as Frankie drained his glass before immediately falling back to sleep, Mollie moved the port out of his reach.

'Max, did you give your mum her present?' She asked, suddenly realising that Tiffany was the only one who was minus a gift. 'I left it on the bookshelf.'

Leaning over Mrs Heckles, Max plucked a silver envelope off the pile of Christmas cards and passed it down the line of people to his mother.

'Merry Christmas, Mum.'

'I was beginning to think I'd been put on the naughty list!'

Tiffany said, politely accepting the envelope and immediately tearing into it. 'It's a gift certificate. For a *very* nice spa.'

A series of appreciative comments passed around the room while Tiffany stared at the gift voucher in silence.

'Is everything okay, Tiff?' Mollie asked, sensing some hesitation. 'Don't you like that place?'

'I *love* this place.' Tiffany replied. 'It's just that...'

'Just what?' Max pressed. 'Even *you* can't want to return that.'

'No, I don't want to return it. I just think there are some people out there who would appreciate this a heck of a lot more than I would.' She admitted, tapping the voucher against her hand. 'Which is why I would like to donate it to the charity Eugenie was telling me about. If that is okay with you two?'

Being the type of woman who went for massages as part of her normal weekly routine, Mollie knew that the offer of a spa treatment wasn't going to blow her mind, but the fact that Tiffany would actually donate her Christmas gift to someone in greater need brought a lump to Mollie's throat.

'You would really do that?' Max asked, placing a hand on his mother's forehead to check her temperature. 'Are you feeling okay?'

'I really would.' Tiff replied. 'You won't catch me shovelling driveways anytime soon, but consider it my contribution to what is quite clearly a fabulous scheme.'

'Tiff!' Completely touched by her mother-in-law's kind gesture, Mollie placed her right hand over her heart. 'What a lovely thing to do! The charity has an auction coming up in the new year, so this will be very gratefully received.'

Blushing at Mollie's praise, Tiffany held out the voucher.

'Just take it before I change my mind.' She demanded, causing Max to whip the envelope out of her hand before she really did have a change of heart. 'There. Good deed done for the day.'

As Eugenie seized the opportunity to wax lyrical about how thankful the Rainbow Volunteer Group would be for Tiff's donation, Mollie caught Tiffany's eye and smiled. It seemed the ice queen had a conscience hiding in there after all.

'You haven't opened your gifts yet, Molls.' Tim said,

pointing to the pile of unopened presents. 'If you don't open them soon, Santa might take them back.'

Pushing herself up, Mollie sat down on the carpet and plucked a gift at random.

'Let's see. This one is from... Joyce.'

In true Joyce style the wrapping paper was completely black, giving no clues as to what was inside. Carefully removing the many layers of Sellotape, Mollie grinned as the rest of the group looked on. Due to Joyce's overzealous wrapping skills, Mollie's gentle attempts proved fruitless and she soon resorted to tearing off the paper like a savage racoon.

'It's a... subscription to Ancestors.' Mollie said, trying to hide her confusion as she read the label. *'The UK's number one ancestry site.* Thank you, Joyce.'

Nodding enthusiastically, Joyce placed her bottle of cider on the coffee table and sprang to life.

'It's actually my own subscription, but I've put my password in there so that you can use it at your leisure.' She explained. 'I thought it would be a good way for you to catch up with the obituaries. It goes all the way back to when records began, so you will be able to see who passed away on your birthday back in the eighteen-hundreds.'

A stunned silence fell over Mollie's living room as the rest of the guests turned to stare at Joyce cautiously. Being very aware of Joyce's morbid fascination with keeping up to date with the deaths that occurred on her birthday, the gift made perfect sense to Mollie.

'I can honestly say, Joyce, I never saw this coming.' She said, allowing a laugh to escape her lips. 'Thank you very much.'

'I could formulate a spreadsheet for us to go back through the years on our lunch breaks.' Joyce offered eagerly. 'It would certainly liven up the cold winter that lies ahead.'

'Spreadsheets?' Kenny scoffed. 'Spreadsheets couldn't liven up a cemetery. You need to spend some more time with us...'

Lost for words, Mollie resorted to a polite smile and moved on to the next gift as Kenny listed the many ways in which Joyce could add some spice to her life in the coming dreary months. From fluffy pyjamas and cosy slippers to plush dressing gowns and woolly mittens, it was safe to say that Mollie wouldn't be needing any spreadsheets to keep her warm.

'Well, I have been completely and utterly spoilt.' She said, looking at the sea of wrapping paper that was surrounding her on the floor. 'Thank you all so very much. I love you all. Even you, Kenny.'

Yet another round of laughter passed around the group as Kenny balled his hands into a pair of chubby fists.

'Mollie?' Mrs Heckles said, tapping Mollie's leg with her walking stick. 'I think you might have missed one...'

Following Mrs Heckles' gaze, Mollie smiled when she spotted a silver box hiding beneath the branches of the Christmas tree.

'So I have.' Mollie said, reaching for the gift box. 'Maybe I've saved the best for last.'

Brushing her hair out of her face, Mollie removed the lid to reveal a red jewellery box. The delicate gold edging twinkled brightly, despite being covered in a thin layer of dust. Fumbling with the clasp, Mollie gasped when she pulled back the lid to reveal a stunning vintage watch. The rectangle face and intricate link bracelet took Mollie's breath away as she looked up at Mrs Heckles in shock, completely lost for words.

'Now, before you say that you can't accept it, I want you to know that you're the closest thing to a daughter I will ever have.' Mrs Heckles said, her smile growing with each word that passed her lips. 'You do more for me than any other human being on this planet ever has.'

A surge of emotion caused Mollie's throat to become uncomfortably tight as she smiled back at her good friend.

'The joy you have brought to my life is absolutely priceless. You have given me a reason to laugh. Most of the time with, but sometimes at.' Turning her attention to Heather and Lawrence, Mrs Heckles' voice cracked slightly. 'She's a credit to you. You should be very proud.'

Mollie's parents beamed with pride as Mollie pushed herself up and wrapped her arms around an emotional Mrs Heckles. They say the best gifts of all are the ones you least expect, and Mrs Heckles' surprise gift had completely floored Mollie. Not because of the value, but because of the incredible sentiment behind it.

'Anyway...' Mrs Heckles said brusquely, snapping back to her usual feisty self. 'It's almost midnight and I still haven't had a rum tea. Who's joining me?'

To Mollie's surprise, everyone in the room nodded in agreement.

'Alright then!' Mollie cheered, heading for the kitchen. 'Rum teas all around!'

'I'll give you a hand.' Jumping to her feet, Heather followed Mollie out of the living room. 'I hope you have enough cups.'

'Luckily, I pre-empted this situation and I've already raided Mrs Heckles' cabinets.' Pulling open various cupboards, Mollie lined up a mismatched collection of cups on the kitchen counter. 'There we go. Just enough.'

Filling up the kettle, Heather sighed loudly and leaned against the sink as Mollie popped a teabag into each one of the cups.

'You know, Mollie, you have no idea how proud it makes me to hear Mrs Heckles talk so highly of you.' She said, reaching out and touching Mollie's cheek with her spare hand. 'Knowing that you're a good friend and neighbour is the best Christmas gift your father and I could ever receive.'

'That's so lovely, Mum, but I *might* be able to do one better...' Holding up a finger to build the suspense, Mollie reached into her back pocket and produced an envelope identical to the one she gave to Tiffany. 'Ta-dah!'

'But you've already given me a gift.' Heather said, pointing to her DIY earrings.

'This one has nothing to do with me.' Mollie replied. 'Santa must have dropped it down the chimney for you.'

Placing the kettle back onto the base to boil, Heather opened the envelope and squealed out loud.

'Claridge's!' She shrieked, her eyes as wide as saucers. 'Really?'

'Really!' Mollie confirmed. 'I promised I would take you to Claridge's one day, didn't I?'

Jumping up and down on the spot, Heather stamped her feet like a child who had just received that year's must-have toy.

'Merry Christmas, Mum.' Laughing at her mother's dramatic reaction, Mollie held out her arms for a hug.

'Oh, Merry Christmas, Mollie.' Heather cried, throwing herself at Mollie. 'Thank you! Thank you so much!'

Wrapping her arms around her mum, Mollie closed her eyes as a wave of content washed over her. Christmas isn't about the number of gifts you receive, it's about the gifts that take your breath away. The price is irrelevant and the packaging meaningless. Happiness and joy simply cannot be measured by the numbers on a receipt. The look on the receiver's face tells you the true value of the gift, whether it cost pennies or pounds.

The sound of the kettle hitting boiling point broke the spell as Mollie finally released Heather and clapped her hands together.

'Alright!' She said, reaching for the kettle and pouring an identical amount of water into each cup. 'Mrs Heckles is very specific about how this is done. Seven stirs anticlockwise, and don't even try testing her because she can sniff out a clockwise stir from a mile away.'

'Anticlockwise.' Heather repeated. 'And the rum goes in...'

'Last of all.' Mollie instructed, adding a touch of milk to each cup. 'And if your hand happens to slip, it's not necessarily a bad thing.'

'Gotcha.'

Shooting Mollie a wink, Heather distributed generous splashes of rum amongst the row of odd cups as Mollie produced a couple of serving trays.

'Are we good to go?' Heather asked, standing back while Mollie loaded up the trays.

Giving her mother the thumbs-up sign, Mollie grabbed a tray and smiled before heading back into the living room. Throwing the perfect Christmas isn't about following a set of tried and tested rituals, because the template for the perfect Christmas doesn't exist. It's as simple as doing whatever makes you happy with whoever you love the most, which is why Mollie McQueen had *not* ruined Christmas.

'Alright, who wants a cuppa?'

To be continued...

Have you read the other books in the Mollie McQueen series?

Mollie McQueen is NOT Getting Divorced

Whoever said money can't buy happiness, obviously never paid for a divorce...

When Mollie McQueen turned thirty, she awoke with a determination to live her best life.

Her marriage to Max was the first thing to come under scrutiny and on one sexless night in May, Mollie decided that their relationship was over.

However, when a grouchy divorce lawyer convinces Mollie there's a chance she could bow out of this life being eaten alive by a pack of cats, she starts to search for an alternative.

Opening the can of worms that is her marriage makes Mollie realise she might not be as blameless as she initially thought...

Will Mollie be able to rescue her marriage or has the lure of a life without wet towels on the bed turned her head?

One thing is for sure... Mollie McQueen is NOT getting divorced.

Mollie McQueen is NOT Having a Baby

Some women want babies, others just want to sleep like one.

Since completing their marriage counselling with therapist to the stars, Evangelina Hamilton, life in the McQueen household is looking rather cosy indeed.

Max is flying high in his new career and Mollie is finally turning her attention to renovating the house that is falling down around them.

Forming an unlikely friendship with none other than the office pariah, Timothy Slease, results in Mollie making it her mission to help him find love.

With a house to renovate and Tim's love life to sprinkle Cupid dust over, the shock of a possible pregnancy hits Mollie harder than a Ronda Rousey left hook.

Not being the type of woman who goes weak at the knees at the sight of a dirty nappy, Mollie resorts to her old coping mechanism of burying her head in the sand.

Picturing her life with a child in tow makes Mollie question everything she was previously so sure of.

With Aunt Flo refusing to play ball, house renovation catastrophes and dating disasters might not be the only things that Mollie McQueen is expecting...

Mollie McQueen is NOT Having Botox

Maybe she was born with it, maybe it's Botox...

It's November. Mollie's least favourite time of the year. The days are short and the nights are cold, but when her nearest and dearest get hit with a case of the midlife crisis bug, it gives her something more than the terrible weather to complain about.

Watching her parents and in-laws putting themselves through chemical peels and hair transplants causes Mollie to make it her mission to prove that the natural approach to anti-aging is best.

Spending time with her eccentric and outlandish neighbour, Mrs Heckles, just adds to Mollie's firm opinion that growing old gracefully is the only attitude to have.

Enlisting the help of Tim's ageless girlfriend, can Mollie convince her loved ones to step away from the scalpel and learn to love the person in the mirror?

With snails, urine and some rather unorthodox tools at her disposal, Mollie certainly has a hard task on her hands, but with a troublesome cat, a huge work opportunity and a friend heading for heartache, will they all be taught a lesson in the cruellest way possible?

One thing is for sure, Mollie McQueen is NOT Having Botox.

Follow Lacey London on Twitter
@thelaceylondon

Printed in Great Britain
by Amazon

51629081R00095